INFLUENCER ISLAND

A NOVEL

KYLE RUTKIN

Published by Greater Path LLC

Cover design by Anamaria Stefan

ISBN: 978-0-9836833-6-0(Paperback)

Thank you BookTok & Bookstagram for renewing my faith in publishing.
Thank you for taking chances on unknown authors.

[PART 1]

SUBMIT YOUR APPLICATIONS

EPISODE ONE:

THE CONTEST

AUDIO CLIP [@SAMMIBARRLOW]: It's been forty-eight hours and we are still being held hostage. There are men with ski masks and guns outside the camp. If you consider yourself one of my fans, please… share this, make sure the public knows what is happening.

AUDIO CLIP [@KIKIKELLY]: [BREATHING HEAVILY] They are going to kill us . . . They are going to kill us all. Please. I beg you. Don't come to the island. It's a trap. **[AUDIO CUTS OUT]**

AUDIO CLIP [@CARRIEANDREWS]: Whoever's watching this, you need to know I'm not a murderer. I'm not a killer. **[PAUSES]** I did what I needed to do to survive.

NBC NEWS AUDIO CLIP: Influencer Island, the social media contest that swept the nation, is now being deemed a catastrophic event as the FBI tries to piece together what exactly happened on the mysterious island in the Bahamas.

BUZZFEED NEWS AUDIO CLIP: The contest, now referred to by the internet as Fyre Festival meets *The Hunger Games*, has gotten the attention of the Federal Bureau of Investigation, who is calling for the immediate arrest of its creator, infamous street artist, Wyatt James.

CNN NEWS AUDIO CLIP: As videos of abducted influencers and murdered contestants continue to go viral, the world awaits some sort of conclusion to the carnage. Will we ever know what happened to the missing models and contestants that came to the island? Time will tell.

CAL: It was marketed as a dream-like event, an opportunity to compete for social media glory, to party with the biggest influencers in the world. For a select few, Influencer Island was a transformative experience as promised. For others, a horrible nightmare that would cost them their lives. Regardless of your opinion, you can't argue its virality, with dozens of trending hashtags, eight million submissions, and perhaps the most enticing promotional video ever created. But at the end of the day, was any of it real?

My name is Cal Everett, executive producer of this podcast. If you're listening, chances are you are one of the 38 million viewers that tuned in to the competition. Three days of euphoric parties, deadly challenges, perilous drug trips, and a possible serial killer set loose on the island. And just as the contest was nearing its tragic conclusion, the feed went dark. No explanation of what happened to any of the murdered or surviving influencers.

Until now.

It was a warm Sunday afternoon, less than twenty-four hours after the contest live feed abruptly ended when FBI Agent Michelle Cooper landed on the tarmac of a privately owned island nicknamed Devil's Cay, one of seven hundred islands that comprise the Bahamas. They were the first team to arrive, tasked with assessing the damage and investigating the tragedy.

AGENT COOPER: Re-watching the footage on the way over, I knew we had our work cut out for us. We had at least nine murder victims, fifty online celebrities being held hostage, thirteen that were still missing, and from those early reports, no sign of the man responsible.

Our first mission was to release the survivors from the Influencer Camp, a small sandbar that was caged in with electric fencing and barbed wire. Most of these kids were in bad shape, living in their own filth for four days straight. Thankfully, other than dehydration and emotional anguish, none of them were seriously injured. After that, my team went looking for the others.

We discovered the first body down at the beach, a corpse that washed up onshore. She was a slender twenty-something, wearing nothing but a string bikini. Her hair and face were matted in seaweed and sand, with black kelp flies buzzing about. The deep gash in the middle of her chest clearly suggested foul play. When I removed the seaweed from her face, I found that the victim's eyes were removed from the sockets. And that's not even the most bizarre thing about the crime scene. There was a painting, a beautiful portrait of the woman on an easel ten feet from the body. She was alive in the portrait, solemnly gazing off in the distance. Covering her eyes was a blurred gold streak. That was the signature mark of the artist, the contest creator, and top of the most wanted list, Wyatt James.

Your report mentions a second body discovered nearby?

From the shore, one of my agents spotted a rusted metal cage swaying from a protruding rock on the cliff. Upon closer inspection, we found the mutilated body of a thirty-something male. He wore a yellow blindfold over his eyes and parts of his flesh were stripped down to the bone.

At the time, did you have any idea why these people were murdered?

Depends on who you ask. There are some online fanatics who believed that Wyatt James was a groundbreaking artist. That this contest was his greatest masterpiece, an art installation that blurred the lines between fiction and reality. Others believe he was a serial killer, plain and simple. In my opinion, the truth is much more complex. If I'm being honest, this case keeps me up at night. Sometimes, I feel like I never left the island. I hope your podcast can give the victims' families and friends some closure, some conclusion to all this.

CAL: Welcome to *Influencer Island*, a podcast that will expose the truth about the catastrophic social media competition. What happened to the murdered victims and the influencers that disappeared? Will the killers be held accountable? Did anyone actually win the contest? Why did Wyatt James create this barbaric installation in the first place? And how did a 24-year old aspiring influencer from Orange County become the key to unlocking everything?

A quick disclaimer before we begin. At times, I have been unethical and callous in my pursuit of the truth. I have violated many of the journalistic standards that our producers at BlueLA Studios strive to uphold. I've lied. I've broken rules. I've put my team in compromising positions. For all of this, I'm truly sorry. As you will soon find out, I allowed my emotions to interfere with my judgment and integrity. Still, if anyone were to finish this story and give the world the answers it deserves, it must be me. That reason will become abundantly clear later.

To tell this story properly, we'll need to start a month prior to the competition.

It was late in the evening at the BlueLA headquarters, a converted industrial building in Venice Beach, California. Our office is the cliché hipster workplace, with open ceilings, graffitied walls, and a luxury espresso bar to keep our sixty-person staff caffeinated into the night. My assistant producer, Joss Solano, and I were sprawled out on beanbag chairs, combing the darkest corners of the internet for our next big story. We didn't have to search long. At 9:47 p.m., a Google Alert pinged on my computer. The news shocked me to my core. Legendary street artist Wyatt James had emerged from hiding.

Here's Joss to tell you about my reaction.

JOSS: His reaction? I've never seen a grown man squeal like that.

CAL: The truth is, I've been obsessed with Wyatt James since his very first installation.

NBC NEWS AUDIO CLIP (2015): A street artist named Wyatt James, referred to in many circles as the Hollywood Banksy, has created quite a frenzy across Los Angeles with his newest art installation entitled Died Famous . . .

CBS NEWS AUDIO CLIP (2015): On his website, the artist claims to have created forty portraits across the Los Angeles landscape, including replacing all three O's on the Hollywood sign with provocative faces of Marilyn Monroe. The various street portraits, all depicting dead celebrities with a golden blur across the eyes, have ignited an Easter egg hunt and media circus across the city.

CAL: I was twenty when Wyatt James emerged on the scene. Just like the rest of Wyatt's admirers, I scrambled from one installation to the next, desperate for a glimpse of his newest piece before authorities took it down—or worse, someone defaced it. The first piece I witnessed in person was *Superfame*, a lifelike plastic dummy of *Superman* actor Christopher Reeves hanging off the Warner Brothers water tower, clad in his iconic red and blue costume, a yellow hood over his head. "Fame is kryptonite" was written in black spray paint across the studio logo.

At least five hundred kids were standing below that water tower, thrilled to snag a picture and share it online. Wyatt was changing the way people consumed art. Here's UCLA Art History professor Dr. Arnie Katz to discuss.

DR. KATZ: The traditional art world had a tough time digesting Wyatt's success. Most of my peers found his work trite and insensitive. But when his Kurt Cobain piece, a six-foot portrait excavated from a rundown donut shop in downtown Los Angeles, sold for three million dollars, they were forced to take him seriously.

CAL: From then on, Wyatt's name became synonymous with celebrity culture—even though the artist himself was a recluse. For the next few years, he produced innovative portraits of the Hollywood elite, both living and deceased. On bus benches and baseball stadium walls. On the Roosevelt Hotel sign and the top of the iconic Capitol Records building. Always with a golden blur across the eyes. Anyone who's anyone in Hollywood wanted to become Wyatt's next muse.

Lane Davis, a reporter at celebrity gossip site TheInsideJuice.com, followed the frenzy.

LANE: Having Wyatt James do your portrait solidified your fame. To many, it was better than any Oscar or Grammy, better than a star on Hollywood Boulevard. I once heard a rumor that Kanye offered him twenty million dollars to paint his portrait. Apparently, Wyatt declined.

CAL: Every celebrity whose likeness was captured by James chronicled a similar experience. They were given a time and place, then James would arrive in all black with a ratty gold ski mask with sharpie'd symbols written all over the cloth. He would ask each subject to wear a blindfold and assume a position. He would spend roughly forty-five minutes painting before he vanished into the night.

Reality television star Kim Kardashian was asked to show up at the abandoned Hawthorne Mall in El Segundo at midnight. Actor Johnny Depp was summoned to a homeless encampment next to the Hollywood Walk of Fame. There was little interaction with the artist. No chitchat. Every subject described the experience as eerie but exhilarating. Wyatt always took one photo of his work before he left, posting it on his Gl!tch account with no caption. The art spoke for itself.

LANE: And then, two years later, came Wyatt's next installation. No one was prepared for what was to come.

NBC NEWS AUDIO CLIP (2017): It seems that controversial street artist Wyatt James is in hot water with authorities for his involvement in a celebrity death.

CAL: Over a three-year timespan, James created seven portraits of celebrities who were later discovered dead on the same day the portraits were released. Even more alarming, the paintings were accompanied by sound bites on Wyatt's website, which he claims to have been recorded on the night before each celebrity allegedly took their own life. Here's an audio clip from Wyatt's final subject in the DIED FAMOUS series, pop star Kelly Trozzo.

AUDIO CLIP OF DECEASED SUPERSTAR KELLY TROZ–

ZO: I won't be another girl who died famous. My name will be written in the stars.

LANE: To me, it almost felt as if these fallen celebrities were making the choice to be immortalized by Wyatt James.

DR. KATZ: I found the paintings in that series truly breathtaking. Very evocative of Rembrandt's ability to capture a subject's soul, except James did it without the eyes. It was in the small details of the face, the lines, the subtle expressions. Somehow, James was able to truly "see" that person. As if obscuring the eyes gave him a unique perspective into their inner pain.

CAL: These paintings also turned Wyatt into the most controversial artist of our generation. Was James cashing in on the suffering of these beloved stars? If he possessed knowledge of their impending suicides, why didn't he report them or try to prevent them? Could he have been involved in their deaths in some way?

After the media frenzy and public outcry, James went back into hiding, the mystery of his identity still intact. In fact, over the next few years, the only work James produced was a series titled *The End is Coming*, a collection of digital art pieces depicting pop culture icons in dystopian settings, including Hollywood director Lucas Yuvani on a metal spike. These portraits were the first digital art pieces (or NFTs) to sell for over a million dollars.

LANE: This generation doesn't give a shit about owning traditional paintings anymore. They'd rather buy a digitized tweet from their favorite celebrity. They want collectibles that represent fame, power, and scandal. Wyatt James served at the intersection of all three. Everyone was on pins and needles to see what he would do next.

CAL: Which leads us to the origin of the Google Alert that got my attention. His biggest installation to date. On his website, Wyatt posted a brand-new recording of a dark and ominous voice, which internet memes have likened to the masked *Star Wars* villain, Kylo Ren.

This is where our story truly begins.

AUDIO CLIP FROM WYATT JAMES: For the sake of this project, my name is @WyattJames. I have eighty million followers. I am an artist, famous for my sins. I have partied and lived amongst the deities you worship. All for the false pretenses of art. Each time I painted, the soul of your gods became blurrier and blurrier, a mark of our civilization fading into obscurity.

I took a sabbatical to rediscover my purpose, leaning into the shadows of this world. I did portraits of tyrants and murderers. I longed to experience true evil. For only in the darkness can we see the lantern that guides us forward.

Alas, I come bearing an antidote. A way to purge this poison from our collective soul. I am designing a new installation. With it, I wish to burn all that is false. The water will run red like the hearts on their photos. How far would you be willing to go for fame and followers? Stay tuned for my masterpiece.

CAL: An hour later, a promotional video appeared on Wyatt's Gl!tch account. Aerial shots of a breathtaking tropical island, layered with quick clips of the world's most popular influencers partying beneath thatched huts, taking tequila shots and selfies in their bikinis. Then the camera panned slowly, capturing the influencers running into the water for a midnight swim with the wispy, sensual voiceover of arguably the biggest reality star in America, Kaylyn Jenson.

AUDIO FROM TRAILER: Welcome to Influencer Island, a once-in-a-lifetime experience. If you are selected, you will be taken to paradise to compete and party with the hottest celebrities. One lucky winner will join the ranks of the world's top celebrities. Are you ready to become the next big influencer?

CAL: Then quick snapshots of eleven of the most influential celebrities of our generation filled the screen. A combined follower count of eight hundred million. All of them said only two words.

AUDIO FROM TRAILER:
Bella Allesandra: Join us.
Kiki Kelly: Join us.
Olivia Ray: Join us.
Angel Asher: Join us.

CAL: At the fifty-second mark, Kaylyn returned to the frame in a gold bikini, strutting on a picturesque beach as the sun set, her long black hair waving in the wind.

AUDIO FROM TRAILER [KAYLYN JENSON]: Post a video telling us why you should be selected. In the coming days, we'll be choosing ten lucky contestants to come to the island to party and compete. Good luck and may fame and followers be upon you.

LANE: What's so fascinating is that on Wyatt's website, he essentially warned everyone that the contest was going to be a social experiment—a dark and twisted mindfuck. Then on social media, he painted the island as a paradise for influencers, with curated photos and stylized graphics. The perfect illusion to lure them in. The promo video racked up fifty million views within twenty-four hours. To my point, it didn't matter who Wyatt James was, or his real intent. You put Kaylyn Jenson in a bikini asking people to come hang out on an exclusive island, and you have pandemonium.

CAL: It was clear that Wyatt's video struck at the heart of what this new generation desires. They don't want to grow up and be an astronaut or a doctor. They want followers. They want verified check marks. They want to be famous.

As soon as I watched the video, I threw down my headphones and marched into my boss's office.

ERIC: I'm Eric Paulson, co-founder of BlueLA Studios. I've seen that look in a reporter's eyes before. This shit was personal for Cal. In hindsight, I should have questioned his motivations before assigning him the gig. That was a mistake.

CAL: Eric gave me the green light to pursue the podcast under a few conditions. He wanted me to find a range of subjects, potential contestants who were willing to let me document their experience. I was told to focus on the motivations of the applicants. While I agreed to Eric's guidelines, I also planned on pursuing another lead from my past. I just wasn't ready to explain to my team why.

JOSS: To be honest, even after Cal got the OK from Eric, I thought the whole thing was going to implode. People couldn't be that stupid, could they? **[LAUGHS]** They could. When I came in the next morning, there were millions of videos posted for us to sift through. All of them seemed like bad opening statements from a Miss America pageant. Cal was so adamant that we needed to find a winning horse to attach our podcast to. It wasn't enough to feature a bizarre and interesting range of subjects. We needed a candidate who Wyatt James would select. A needle in a, dare I say, hashtag haystack.

CONTEST ENTRY AUDIO: My name is Jewell Peters, and I'm ready to disrupt the beauty industry.
CONTEST ENTRY AUDIO: It's your boy Tony here. I got mad skills. I can sing, choreograph, and the ladies love my . . .
CONTEST ENTRY AUDIO: I would die to go on Influencer Island. Seriously. Die. OH MY GOD! I'll do whatever it takes to party with Kaylyn Jenson. ANYTHING! I need to be there! Please pick me!

CAL: Those first few days were rough. My team—Joss, Tony, Amy, and I—lived inside the conference room. We put up a poster board with at least fifty potential subjects. We had fashion influencers. Food influencers. DJs. Poets. But just as we were about to vote, I received an anonymous email. Inside was a link to a video that had gone under the radar. Two twenty-four-year-olds from right here in our own backyard. Their names were Carrie Andrews and Kiana Martin.

The unauthenticated email also had a note attached. It said, *I have reason to believe that these users will be selected by Wyatt James.*

JOSS: So we have this incredible stack of potential subjects, and we're getting ready to vote, when Cal storms in the room and dramatically tears every single photo off the board. Three days of working day and night, guzzling chow mein and energy drinks, and he stapled two basic girls to the wall.

CAL: Looking back, I could have been less theatrical.

JOSS: When Cal played us the video in the conference room, the team stared at each other in shock. *He must be joking.* These girls were batshit crazy. In the video, Carrie drunkenly ranted about her ex-boyfriend on a public toilet while her friend, Kiana, egged her on in the background. They were train wrecks. And then Cal said that he was narrowing the podcast subjects down from five to two.

From our perspective, Carrie and Kiana met none of the criteria we were looking for. Their video had less than ten thousand views. Other than physical looks and Carrie's volatile behavior, there was nothing unique about them. And we were essentially gambling an entire podcast on them.

Finally, we all just caved. Anything to get home and get some sleep.

CAL: What can I say? It was a gut feeling. Whoever sent me that email, was trying to help me. I knew these subjects would lead us to Wyatt James.

CAL: As most of you know, Carrie Andrews ultimately became the final contestant selected for Influencer Island. Sadly, in the days following the contest conclusion, she was the *only* contestant that the FBI found alive. According to Agent Michelle Cooper, Carrie was discovered staggering through the jungle, lost in a state of madness. She had blood all over her; eyes swollen, her hair wild. She was injured badly. There were at least three visible wounds, one of which had been cauterized by an iron brand. Despite her physical state, and the various horrors she had endured, Carrie wasn't treated as a victim. Based on the online footage, and a disturbing selfie-style video confession, Carrie was detained as a suspected murderer. Following her initial interrogation, she was transferred to Guantanamo Bay Detention Center for further questioning while the FBI continued the investigation and searched for survivors.

From the moment I was notified of Carrie's detainment, I began petitioning the FBI to grant me access. Whether it was guilt, or my own personal relationship with the subject, I couldn't eat or sleep knowing that she was confined to a prison cell. Using every platform at my disposal, I lobbied authorities for her extradition back home.

By then, it had been over a week since the contest ended and the public was in an absolute uproar. Nine people were declared dead, and eleven influencers were still missing. The FBI had not made a statement in four days, and my boss was at his wit's end. He had waited long enough for me to release the podcast. In fact, I was just about to announce a launch date, when I received a phone call from FBI Director Mark Sanchez. He said, "Carrie Andrews has asked to speak with you. You are the only one she will talk to."

Within twenty-four hours, Joss and I arrived at Guantanamo Bay Naval Base in Cuba. Agent Cooper greeted us on the helicopter pad. She was wearing her FBI windbreaker and high-waisted khaki pants, with dark sunglasses and a springy ponytail. As we walked, she told us about an anonymous tip she received. Evidently, one of the missing contestants (identity unknown) was spotted wandering the streets of Havana. Although Agent Cooper had no idea how the contestant got there, nor any information about the other missing influencers, she was optimistic they would turn up soon.

As we made our way through the detention center's maze of metal fences, my chest tightened with nerves. After everything Carrie went through, I had no idea what to expect. Would there be any remnant of the girl I met at the beginning of this journey?

We were brought to a concrete room with a one-way mirror into an interrogation cell. Within minutes, Carrie was escorted into the cell by two military guards. It was unsettling to see her in this state, dressed in a baggy prison jumpsuit, handcuffs around her wrists. She didn't look well. Her face was pale and drained, her blonde hair unkempt and frizzled.

Before I walked in, Joss gave me a pep talk: *Stay strong, stay on point.* We both knew that Carrie's testimony was the key to unlocking the secrets of Influencer Island, and from a journalistic point of view, this wasn't an ideal situation. Would I let my personal relationship with the subject interfere? Would I ask the hard questions when it came down to it? Could I get her to admit the truth of her role in all this?

As soon as I was buzzed in, Carrie glanced up from the metal table. Her blue eyes were a shade darker, her face rigid and callous. This woman had done unspeakable things. She'd already confessed to killing multiple individuals. Despite that, I couldn't help my feelings from flooding back. Beneath the distressed surface, the girl I fell in love with was still there. I sat down across from her and pushed play on the recorder.

How are you?

CARRIE: I've been better.

Can you state your full name for the record?

Carrie Alice Andrews.

Two months ago, I approached you and Kiana Martin to be subjects for a new podcast about Influencer Island?

That's correct.

Why did you two agree to be the subject of the podcast?

I wanted to bring more attention to my brother's missing person case. I never thought we had a chance to be selected.

And why have you agreed to this interview?

The world needs to know the truth. What they saw on the island was only part of the story. They need to know why I did the things I did. Mostly, I need them to know why he chose me.

Things you did? Are you referring to the murder of three of your fellow contestants?

I brought you here so I could tell *my* truth. The whole truth. They don't know half of what Wyatt James put us through. They don't know who I am. You don't know the things I've seen. The horrors I've experienced. **[PAUSES, LOOKS DOWN]** When I close my eyes, I can still see them. I can still feel their warm blood splashing across my hands. Their frightened faces staring back at me. I did horrible things. Unspeakable things. I'm not the same girl that you met in that café a month ago. The island changed me. I need you and everyone to understand how. I need you to know what he did to us. Why he did it. And what I had to do to survive.

EPISODE TWO:

THE SURFER

THREE WEEKS PRIOR TO THE CONTEST

CAL: It was a sunny day in Newport Beach when Joss and I walked into Kip's, a hipster hideaway with six-dollar oat milk lattes and elevated avocado toast. Everyone there had tattoos and baggy clothing, working from a shiny MacBook or journaling in a Moleskin notebook. The clickety clack of Apple keyboards and the hiss of oat milk being steamed echoed through the café.

This was our first official interview with Carrie and Kiana, and I was eager to get started. It was a week before contestants would be announced, and if this mysterious email was correct, these aspiring influencers would lead us to Wyatt James. I was betting everything on them.

Carrie and Kiana bore little resemblance to the drunken girls in their submission video. They were both stunning. Carrie had a post-beach glow about her, perfectly tanned skin, subtle makeup, a small patch of freckles under her left eye. Kiana had a bit more edge, with jet black hair, a nose ring and tattoo sleeve. While Carrie sported high waisted jeans and a crop top, Kiana wore an oversized shirt and chunky Doc Martens.

According to our pre-interview notes, the two had been insepa-rable since they were six years old. I asked the girls about their mental state in the hours leading up to their video submission. What motivated Carrie to post such a personal video from a public toilet?

CARRIE: I was in a bad place that night. It was the one-year anniversary of my brother's disappearance.

CAL: Carrie was referring to Tuck Andrews, a 29-year-old surf instructor, who spent three years in and out of rehab before he was reported missing last year. During the investigation, it was determined that Tuck's last-known location was a rave called Wonderland, which took place in an abandoned printing factory in Orange County. According to Carrie, no witnesses ever came forth with additional information.

CARRIE: He was my big brother. He was the one who raised me. He taught me what music to like. **[SMILES]** Mostly garage and punk rock. What books to read. More importantly, he taught me how to surf. His buddies used to tease him for letting his little sister tag along on their surf outings. Tuck used to tell them, "Just wait. She'll be surfing laps around you idiots one day." And he was right. My brother was the only person who's ever believed in me.

On the night I posted my submission video, I was scrolling through old photos of Tuck on my camera roll. I was staring at one in particular, taken at the US Open of Surfing, where I beat out the number one surfer at the time, Angel Asher. In the picture, I was hoisted on Tuck's bony shoulders, holding up the trophy. It was the pinnacle of my career. It was the best day of our lives. **[TAKES A DEEP BREATH]**

Minutes later, I was back on Gl!tch where I saw Wyatt's post. It was everywhere by then. The only thing anyone was taking about. And guess who was a featured influencer in that video? The surfer I beat that day, Angel Asher.

CAL: A lot happened since Carrie first beat Angel on the beaches of Huntington. Carrie tore her knee in a bad surf accident, quit the professional surfing circuit, and ended up waitressing at a local vegan restaurant. And Angel . . . She was the "it" girl in the surfer influencer community.

CARRIE: Angel Asher lived this amazing life. Millions of followers. Sponsorship deals. Free trips to every surfing hotspot in the world. Partying with Wyatt James on an exclusive island. It didn't matter that she hadn't won a pro event since we were teenagers. She was beyond gorgeous and wore bikini bottoms the size of a shoelace. That was all that mattered on Gl!tch.

CAL: Then Carrie recalled scrolling to her own account.

CARRIE: I was a nobody. Less than six thousand followers. Most of them were thirsty guys I'd never met. And I began to wonder: *What would it be like to be Angel Asher?* To have millions of fans adore me. To have brands throw money at me just to mention their name. To be paid to travel around the world and take pictures in a bikini. What would my life be like if I hadn't gotten injured? Maybe I wouldn't be stuck in Newport Beach. Stuck in some fake, plastic town that reminded me of my brother at every turn. Kiana and I were meant for bigger things.

KIANA: I was supposed to be a singer. It was in my blood. My late father was a jazz musician, and his father was too. I paid my dues in dive bars for years before getting my "lucky break," a six-city tour as the opener for Halsey. But right before the first show, my manager fucked up the deal, and got me dropped from my label. All my hard work...gone in seconds. Both Carrie and I were handed shitty deals.

And that's why you entered the contest?

KIANA: As you saw in the video, Carrie was pretty hammered that night... If I'm being honest, that was Carrie on most nights. Ever since Tuck went missing. She doesn't have an off button. I usually drag her home before she hooks up with a rando. I tried to call an Uber that night, but Carrie was on another level.

Because it was the anniversary of your brother's disappearance?

CARRIE: Not just that. We also ran into my ex, Chad, and his new girlfriend.

KIANA: In Carrie's defense, the guy drained half of her savings so he could surf and get shitfaced with his wannabe band. He was a real piece of work. And according to his annoyingly younger girlfriend, he had some amazing job in finance. They were totally rubbing it in Carrie's face.

CARRIE: I hated the way they stared at me. With pity. Like I was some loser who hadn't done anything with my life. Like I threw away so much potential. So, I decided to drown my sorrows in tequila. According to Kiana, I was in rare form. Dancing on the bar top. Picking a fight with the bartender. By midnight, I was in a bathroom stall hugging the porcelain goddess.

KIANA: I was in the next stall over when I heard the new girlfriend barge in with her friends to put on makeup. They were going on and on about her entry for Influencer Island. How she was some wellness creator that was going to make a difference in the world. Bunch of bullshit like that. Then she told her friend that she ran into Chad's ex girlfriend. She said something like, "She used to be like a pro-surfer. Now she's like... a total loser."

CARRIE: My brother raised me to be a competitor. I could almost hear his voice in my head: *Are you really going to let this snotty little shit beat you?*

CAL: And that's when Carrie and Kiana turned their camera around and shot their unorthodox submission video. A video that would change their life forever.

CAL: Now that we've introduced you to Carrie and Kiana, there's another influencer you'll need to meet. Her name is Bella Allesandra, and with 28 million followers she is one of the top models and influencers in the world. She was also one of the original eleven models that went to the island to promote the contest.

LANE DAVIS, THEINSIDEJUICE.COM: Hands down, Bella Allesandra is one of the savviest and wealthiest influencers in the business. She's someone who's mastered personal branding, with her neon makeup palette, colorful fashion, and that signature lavender streak running through her long black hair. It doesn't hurt that she's blessed with good looks and a curvaceous body, which she gladly showcases online.

CAL: By the time Bella was rescued by the FBI, the flawless, charismatic influencer that the world had come to know was hardly recognizable. In a picture that has since gone viral, a traumatized Bella is seen being dragged out of a hole in the ground without makeup, covered in dirt, her black hair matted, wearing nothing but a grimy jumpsuit. What you are about to hear is the FBI recording of Allesandra's debriefing three days after the contest ended.

BELLA ALLESANDRA: [FBI AUDIO RECORDING]

Can you please state your name and why you are here?

My name is Bella Allesandra. I've been held against my will on this island for weeks.

Do you know where the rest of the influencers are?

They were kidnapped by the devil himself. **[LEANS BACK, SCOWLS]** I'm not sure why you are talking to me. You should be out there looking for their bodies.

Trust us, we are doing everything in our power to find them. That's why we need you. We need to know everything about

Wyatt's plans. How about we start at the beginning. Can you tell us how you were invited to the island?

[SNICKERS] How could I forget an invitation like that? I was sunbathing at a hotel pool in the French Riviera when I received a text from my manager, Billy Atlas. He claimed that Wyatt James sent me an NFT, a piece of digital art, as a gift. This was right when digital art was hitting mainstream. I was ecstatic to get something like this from an artist like Wyatt. We all were. His stuff was selling for millions. He was a big fucking deal.

What was the art piece?

The thumbnail was a 3D animated envelope with a red seal, and some creepy skull embedded into the wax. It was numbered one out of eleven. But there was a catch. If you accepted the gift, you accepted his invitation. As if it were a binding contract. I didn't hesitate. I wanted whatever Wyatt James had to offer. Once the letter opened up, the frame turned black, and seconds later, Wyatt's face appeared on the screen. The whole thing was disturbing, with that ratchet ski mask and hollowed-out eyes floating on my laptop. Then came that mechanical, demonic voice of his.

He said he was putting on a new installation. He invited me to come to the island and audition to become one of his disciples. He would pay me five million dollars for three weeks' worth of work. He told me to be at a private hangar in Los Angeles at 4:00 p.m., a week from that day.

So you accepted, no questions asked?

I wasn't raised with a silver spoon. I'm second generation, Israeli-American. My parents made it in this country with hard work and determination. So don't lump me in with the rest of those privileged girls. I'm not some dimwitted model with no street smarts. I was fifteen when I started in this business, and I never had Mommy and Daddy fetching me water in-between takes. But this was Wyatt James. He was friends with the biggest celebrities in the world. He had a verified fucking check mark. This was five million dollars. Even if it turned out to be some bizarre shit, I could handle it. Tell me you wouldn't do the same? **[PAUSES, TAPPING HER NAILS AGAINST THE TABLE]**

I endured that monster. I outlasted all the others. I was the only one who didn't succumb. You'll see. You'll see. Now, can someone please get me some fucking water?

CAL: Most likely you already have your opinion about Wyatt James. Whether he is indeed a monster or a mad genius. Who is Wyatt James? That's a riddle I've been trying to solve for years.

It was 2017 and I had dropped out of art school. While most of my peers graduated and continued their artistic careers, I chose to abandon my dream of becoming a painter. Instead, I decided to become an investigative journalist. While the next logical step would have been to get a job or an internship with a news organization, I took a more entrepreneurial approach. I spent my own savings to chase down a real story. I vowed to uncover the true identity of Wyatt James.

With no experience or direction, I chased hundreds of leads—anyone who had seen a masked figure painting in Los Angeles around the time of his first installations. I read hundreds of forums and Reddit threads, trawling the web for clues. I even hired a tech guy to try to hack Wyatt World, an archaic online forum for Wyatt fanatics. No luck. But just when things were looking grim, I finally got my lucky break. An email showed up from a Hollywood insider who claimed he had information for me. Here's an old recording of that interview.

AUDIO FROM MIKE WALLER INTERVIEW: I was a production assistant in Hollywood for a decade. I like to think that I was one of the first people to ever witness a Wyatt James painting. I was on my lunch break on the

Warner Brothers backlot when I spotted a bunch of people hanging around Studio Twenty. When I approached, I saw a portrait graffitied on the exterior wall. The subject was Warner Brothers studio head Paul Riley, outfitted with a pig nose and a blurred gold line across his eyes.

CAL: The graffiti was painted over within hours. But the logical conclusion was this.

AUDIO FROM MIKE WALLER INTERVIEW: I suspect Wyatt James was an employee—or at least had some sort of affiliation—with Warner Brothers. I believe he was wronged by the studio's CEO at the time, Paul Riley.

CAL: Imagine my excitement: a young, aspiring journalist who'd just stumbled across an unpublicized clue to the true identity of Wyatt James. My obsession grew tenfold. For the next seven months, I turned over every stone, speaking with anyone who had ever been mistreated by the big boss at Warner Brothers. I contacted writers and directors who were fired. Assistants. Baristas near the studio. But once again, I hit a dead end.

By then, it had been almost a year, and my obsession wasn't healthy. My bedroom wall looked like an FBI evidence stringboard you see in the movies. I had no social life, a depleted savings account, and a story that was going nowhere.

Finally, I packed up my box of Wyatt James materials, stuffed it in the garage, and found an opening at BlueLA Studios. For the next few years, I kept my nose down and buried myself in my work. I stayed late, climbed the ladder, and did my best to forget about Wyatt James. At least until the time was right.

So on the night Eric gave me the greenlight to produce this podcast, I opened that old box, eager to pick up where the trail ran cold. My target was former Warner Brothers CEO Paul Riley, who'd refused to talk to me when he was still head of the studio.

But a lot had changed since then…

JOSS: I was under the impression that we were focusing our energy on documenting the journey of two contestant hopefuls. When I asked Cal why he was trying to schedule an interview with the ex-CEO of Warner Brothers, he gave me a vague response. I advised him to stay on track. Listen, Cal's a talented guy. He has great instincts. He worked his ass off to make executive producer. But I couldn't shake the feeling that there was more to this story. He was making one questionable decision after the next. If I had only known his true motives.

CAL: On June 23rd, four days before the Influencer Island promotional video aired, talent manager Billy Atlas became the first to post from the mysterious island. For those who don't know, Atlas was considered the biggest "influencer" manager in the world. In the selfie-style video, Atlas, with his chubby cheeks and slicked back hair, was outfitted in a white linen suit, a cigar in hand, grinning from ear to ear as he held his phone out. This is the last time Billy would be seen alive.

AUDIO FROM BILLY ATLAS'S ACCOUNT: What's up, fam! I'm here on a remote fucking island in the Bahamas with eleven of the hottest models. We got Olivia Ray. Sienna Owens. Kiki Kelly. And of course, the queen Bella Allesandra. Say hi, ladies. **[MODELS CASUALLY WAVE IN THE BACKGROUND]**

Wyatt James, the biggest artist in the world,

has something epic planned. We're making
history out here, y'all!

BELLA ALLESANDRA: Billy talked a big game, but he didn't
know shit. He was just as clueless as the rest of us. We all had our
guesses. Kiki thought we were promoting a new festival. Olivia
thought Wyatt wanted to parade his wealth and power for a
weekend. Pamper us on his yacht.

What did you think?

Worst case? We'd drink blood and hold a chainsaw while Wyatt
James painted us in skimpy ass bathing suits. Wouldn't be the
weirdest job I've ever had. And what did we care? We were being
flown to paradise on a private jet stocked full of Dom Perignon
and caviar.

Things changed once we landed on the tarmac. As soon as Billy
stopped his little video, five military Jeeps with armed men pulled
up. They were wearing gold jumpsuits and yellow ski masks.
They ordered us to hand over our phones and get into the vehi-
cles. The other models were scared shitless. **[SCOFFS]** And it
wasn't like we could call for help. The island was desolate. No
hotel. No houses, nothing. The road into the jungle was bumpy
and barely maintained. Finally, we came to some security check-
point, a barbed-wire fence guarded by masked men with AK-47s.
[LAUGHS] Welcome to Influencer Island.

Our final destination was a campground of fifteen or so tents right
on the edge of a seaside cliff. Two dozen soldiers in the same
uniform moved about the camp. Not a single person showed their
face. It felt like an episode of *Squid Game*. No matter how many
slasher movies you watch, it's impossible to know when you're
starring in one.

The models were escorted straight into the biggest tent in the camp.
Well, everyone except Billy. Wyatt had special plans for him. The tent

was some sort of dining room, with a massive table set for eleven. And towering above it all was this thirty-foot oil painting on an easel. I'll never forget that painting—eleven women in togas standing on a beach. And in the middle of them all was a man wearing a crown of bones. Fucking disturbing. But a forewarning of what was ahead.

Why?

I'll get there. Dinner was served to us on silver platters, a picturesque three-course meal. But you could feel the tension in the room, you know? Like one of those dramatic TV episodes with extended scenes, and you're just waiting for shit to go down. At one point, everyone heard a scream from somewhere in the camp. I'm assuming it was Billy. **[SNICKERS]** The other girls were oblivious. They were drinking and laughing without a care in the world. But then the music stopped, and a dozen or so masked men entered the dining room... That's when I knew we were fucked.

Wyatt James came in next, marching to the head of the table, his gaze fixated on the painting. Using that villainous voice, he recounted the history of the island. It was once called *Isle de Paradiso*, and it was fabled to be the original Eden. Full of wonder, women, and all the riches you desired. But in reality, the island was none of those things. It became home to a menacing pirate, nicknamed King James, a man who wore the bones of his enemies over his scarred face.

According to Wyatt, the pirate king was the first to understand viral marketing. He enlisted a network of disciples to spread stories of the legendary island across the world, to every thirsty sailor willing to listen. When these sailors landed on his shores, King James sent women to lure them to his fortress. Once inside, the disciples would host a big feast and at the end, King James would enter the hall and lock the doors.

As soon as he said that, armed soldiers entered our tent, standing in front of the exits with guns in hand. All the girls started screaming.

Then Wyatt paused.

"King James would raise a glass," Wyatt said, and then he asked us to raise our glasses.

All the girls were hysterical at this point, visibly shaking. We all did what we were told.

I remember the next words so clearly. He said, "When you awake, we shall see who has what it takes to become my true disciples. Your first task will be to lure them all to the island. Make them believe they are coming to paradise. And it shall be the greatest spectacle this world has ever seen."

As he spoke, I could feel my vision start to blur. He had put something in our drinks. Still, I yelled in defiance, "And if we don't?"

Wyatt turned to me and said, "Then you shall die."

As soon as he made the threat, all the girls screamed at the top of their lungs. That was the last thing I remember before everything went black.

EPISODE THREE:

THE VIRAL VIDEO

CAL: It was a Monday morning, five days before the contestants were scheduled to be announced. Besides a slight hangover from a Sunday Funday, Carrie Andrews' morning routine started off the same as always. She threw off her oversized white down comforter and placed her tanned feet into her Ugg slippers. The sun, along with the salty air of the Pacific Ocean, shimmered through the windows. With sleepy eyes, Carrie grabbed her phone and made her way to the kitchen to make coffee.

Most days, she scrolled mindlessly as she dispensed boiling water over pricey coffee grounds. Double tap. Scroll. Double tap. But that morning, when she opened Gl!tch, she gasped, dropping the boiling water to the floor. Even with the hot water seeping through her slippers, Carrie couldn't take her eyes off the screen. Thousands of notifications flooded her phone. She had gone from six thousand to a hundred thousand followers overnight.

A few things happened while Carrie was sleeping off those bottomless mimosas. First, Buzzfeed published a list entitled "The TOP 10 CRINGIEST 'INFLUENCER ISLAND' VIDEOS." Carrie and Kiana's video was at the top. Then supermodel Kristy Townsend shared the video with the caption, "If they go to the island, I'll watch. #LoveAGoodCrazy." From there, the video cata-pulted through the digisphere. By one in the afternoon that Monday, it was trending, racking up over eighteen million views on Gl!tch.

Carrie Andrews and Kiana Martin's stock were on the rise.

ABC NEWS AUDIO CLIP: They are being called the "Bathroom Stall Duo." The Newport Beach natives might not need to go on a gameshow to become famous . . .

BUZZFEED NEWS AUDIO CLIP: The five-minute rant from a bathroom stall of a local nightclub is quickly making them fan favorites to become contestants on Influencer Island.

CARRIE: No one prepares you for that kind of viral fame. I could have done without the toilet seat and graffitied dicks in the back-ground. It was shocking how easily people could call me a slut or privileged whore without knowing anything about me.

What did your parents think?

My parents. **[LAUGHS]** I hardly knew my mother. She died of an aneurism when I was six. My father coped by working 15-hour days and marrying a younger, pill-popping housewife. Like I said, Tuck raised me. He was the one who made my lunches. The one who took me school shopping.

My father disowned Tuck after he got busted for drugs. He was embarrassed by him. So when he got kicked out at seventeen, I moved out with him. I can't tell you how disappointed Tuck would be if he knew my dad wired me money to help out with rent… It kills me. It really fucking kills me. I saw Influencer Island as a way out.

KIANA: I felt the same way. After the video, my EP on Spotify got more streams in a day than in the past three years. I had a ton of new followers and old industry friends reaching out. This was a second chance for me. And this time, I wasn't going to fuck it up.

CAL: To meet the demands of a rising influencer, Kiana dug through old industry contacts and found her former publicist, Linda Lundgreen. As fortune would have it, Linda now ran a social media talent agency. With Influencer Island growing in popularity, taking on Carrie and Kiana as clients was a no brainer.

LINDA: My name is Linda Lundgreen, and I manage some of the top creators and influencers in the world. It's all about personal brand for these kids. They are products we are selling to the masses. Kiana and Carrie came across like hot messes in the video —and not in the relatable way that mommy influencers can get away with. So unless they wanted to brand themselves as trashy Newport party girls, they needed to stylize and polish their feeds. We needed to make Kiana an edgy popstar, and Carrie, a beautiful southern California goddess.

CAL: To make this happen, Linda booked a photoshoot for Kiana and Carrie in Venice Beach and I went along. For Kiana, the pictures focused on the city's downtown area—artsy shots of her playing guitar on the boardwalk, eating a greasy cheeseburger in a beanie and flannel shirt. For Carrie, the backdrop was the shoreline, and the wardrobe was five skimpy thong bikinis. Posing was second nature for Carrie. The hand on her hip, the deep stare, the sensual gaze off into the distance as she gripped her surfboard. As I watched from afar, I couldn't help but think this was all a little ridiculous. But when I glanced around the beach, I noticed at least five other young girls doing the exact same thing, but with iPhones instead of expensive cameras. Were all these kids aspiring to be influencers? It felt like an episode of *Black Mirror*.

After the shoot, everyone went back to Linda's office, and the social media team started putting pictures into a media scheduling platform, adding basic captions to Carrie's account like *"Getting Vitamin Sea"* (yes, like the ocean), and personal growth quotes and emojis to accompany her half-naked poses. As the team talked strategy, I noticed that Carrie wasn't engaging. Her face was drained of color as she stared at her phone. I asked her what was wrong, and Carrie turned her phone around. A pizza shop owner, username @HarrysPizza, posted a picture of Carrie and her brother in front of his store. In the photo, a fifteen-year-old Carrie is standing next to her lanky brother, Tuck Andrews, both holding a slice of pizza. Tuck was a good-looking kid, with a wide smile and the same light blue eyes as Carrie.

I asked Carrie why the photo bothered her so much.

CARRIE: Tuck and I used to go to Harry's after every training session. We'd go over every ride, dissect every wave. The owner gave us free slices. **[LAUGHS]** Tuck promised I'd promote him when I became famous… The photos are a reminder that my brother could still be out there. The LAPD didn't do jack shit to find him. For three months straight, I was the only one searching.

KIANA: You weren't the only one searching. We all loved Tuck.

CARRIE: Sorry, I know you helped. I know you guys were close.

KIANA: Tuck came to every single one of my shows. He supported me in ways my family never did. He had this natural charisma, this spark that everyone wanted to be around. And he was talented. The kind of guy that can hear a song once and then play it back on his guitar. Carrie already knows this, but Tuck was my first crush. When I was in the second grade, I used to sneak into his room and watch him play guitar. In eighth grade, I'd go to his room and ask for a hit of weed… But he loved Carrie. She was his world.

Who reported him missing?

CARRIE: I did. Even after I stopped surfing, he used to text me the local surf report on Sunday. It was our thing. His way of letting me know he was okay. When he didn't text me that Sunday, I knew something was wrong. The police never took it seriously. After three months missing, I went to a dark place. The detectives kept telling me that it was drug related. But I knew better. My brother was on the up. He was getting clean. We were planning on meeting for lunch the following week. He said he had someone special he wanted to tell me about. He was in love. He wouldn't lie to me.

AGENT MICHELLE COOPER: I didn't know anything about the Tuck Andrews case prior to the Influencer Island competition. Once we started piecing the investigation together, it was clear that something sinister was at work. Due to his history of drug abuse, and association with known gang members, it wasn't given adequate attention. Now we know better. His case was the key to unlocking this entire thing.

CAL: That day, I asked Carrie if she'd like me to investigate her brother's disappearance. I remember her glancing down at her phone, staring at her budding social media account. Wondering if she really wanted to go down this road again. How much easier it would be to just dive back into this new world of fame and double taps.

She asked me, "Is this for the podcast or for me?"

I said, "Both."

I wasn't lying. I hate to admit it, but I was beginning to have feelings for Carrie Andrews.

CAL: Meanwhile, I was still chasing leads behind my team's back, most notably, the subject of Wyatt's first painting. Former Warner Brothers CEO Paul Riley invited me to his office in Beverly Hills. A lot had transpired since my first attempt to contact Riley. He'd been caught in a sexual harassment scandal with an assistant and subsequently fired for misconduct. Since then, he became CEO of a tech hardware company. His office was on the seventh floor of a swanky commercial building, with pristine marble floors and glass walls separating the offices—a powerful message to anyone who thought Riley had fallen from grace since his departure from Warner Brothers.

Physically, he fit the part. He was lean and handsome, with a well-tailored suit and a sleek haircut that made him look like Roger Sterling in *Mad Men*.

PAUL RILEY: My name is Paul Riley, and I was the CEO of Warner Brothers Studios from 2010 to 2015. **[NODDING]** Sure, I had enemies. Comes with the job. You have to fire directors, destroy dreams, make tough decisions on what gets made and what gets shelved. Careers were made or ruined on my orders.

CAL: For much of the interview, Riley relived some of his successes, relishing the trip down memory lane. He launched into long, humorous anecdotes about the hit TV shows and movies he helped launch and the awards won during his tenure. Finally, I asked him the question I'd come for.

PAUL RILEY: I remember that ridiculous portrait. **[CHUCKLES TO HIMSELF]** There was a pilot I canceled when I first took over at Warners. My predecessor ordered three episodes of this far-out show. To be fair, it had a clever premise. The show was centered around a struggling husband-and-wife music duo and their eight-year-old daughter. To make ends meet, they open a sandwich shop, and in the back of this mysterious storefront, they find a guitar case that supposedly belonged to one of the Beatles, George Harrison, I think. And inside was a bag of psychedelics.

CAL: Riley said he'd thought the pilot episode was good, but it wasn't exactly primetime material.

PAUL RILEY: The entire premise was based on an acid trip. It was shot in this half animation, half reality style. Very innovative. Very clever. Excellent chemistry between the characters. They must have put a ton of work into this thing. But c'mon. It wasn't primetime.

CAL: As I listened to Riley talk about the show, the question lingered. *Why would he bother telling me about this one random show he canceled?* That's when Riley flipped around his MacBook display to show me a promo poster for the show, *Yellow Sub*. It was a family of three, standing in front of their decrepit sandwich shop. A recognizable blur over the eyes of every family member.

PAUL RILEY: That's right. Wyatt James' signature style originated from this TV pilot ad. It was supposed to be an abstract take on a yellow submarine, an ode to the acid trip premise of the show.

CAL: Whoever Wyatt James was, somehow, he was associated with this show. And when it got canceled, he must have lashed out, blaming the man responsible. I was one step closer to finding Wyatt's true identity.

JOSS: When Cal got back to the office, he was whistling like an idiot. I knew Cal had gone rogue.

LANE: With three days left until the contestants were announced, Influencer Island had captivated the world, thanks to the models who were living on the island. They had been posting some of the most compelling content you could imagine. Posing on the decks of their thatched huts. Twirling their toes in the crystal blue water. Laughing as they chased around the island's wild chickens. The most iconic shot came from supermodel Olivia Ray's account. It was a video of her, Bella Allesandra, and Kiki Kelly in wet bikinis, slowly emerging from the surf, a shipwrecked wartime vessel in the background. The caption read, "Who wants to be shipwrecked with us?" Eighteen million people affirmed with a double tap.

CAL: With Influencer Island endorsed by top online celebrities, the aspiring contestants were reaping the benefits. Carrie Andrews had accumulated 345,000 followers. By internet standards, she was an influencer. She also took her publicist's advice by curating her feed with pristine pictures of herself in a bikini with playful, witty captions and meme-style videos. Kiana Martin's music career was also reignited. The increase in visibility and followers had gotten the attention of her old label and industry contacts. It seemed that Kiana was back in the fold.

As their popularity grew, it became harder and harder to get a hold of the duo. Sometimes, I found myself staring at Carrie's photos, scrolling through her comments, trying to understand this bizarre culture of internet fame. On the surface, Carrie hadn't done anything special. She hadn't won a surf competition. She hadn't started a business. She didn't offer expertise or donate time or money to any social causes. In fact, other than showcasing her physical appearance and documenting her curated life, there was very little substance to her content. And yet, just like the rest of her followers, I was completely enamored, checking my Gl!tch account every thirty minutes to see if she posted anything new.

JOSS: I told fanboy to stop making excuses and get us a follow-up interview. We had a podcast to produce.

CAL: Thankfully, after a dozen VMs, Carrie agreed to let us come to her home for an interview. It was dusk by the time we arrived at her two-bedroom apartment in Newport Beach. Carrie wore a plain white shirt and high waisted jeans with holes in the knees. It was the first time I noticed two thick scars on her knee from her surfing accident.

Carrie lived in a small beachy apartment, close enough to hear waves crashing against the shore. Her décor was modern and clean, with fluffy rugs, reclaimed wood coffee tables, black and white ocean photographs, and a trashcan full of wine bottles.

Carrie told us that this was originally her brother's place. She moved in when she was fifteen, so they could start training full time. As we strolled through her apartment, I noticed several dusty surfboards on the patio, along with a dry, faded wetsuit that hung from the rafters. From the look of it, she hadn't surfed in quite some time.

The last stop on the tour was Tuck's old bedroom. Besides an air mattress that Kiana crashed on from time to time, the room was bare. Inside the closet was all of Tuck's belongings—clothes, guitars, crates of notebooks. Carrie admitted that it was too difficult for her to go through his old stuff. But she gave us the green-light to browse.

Based on his belongings, Tuck was quite the artist. We found at least fifty notebooks of his sketches, doodles, music lyrics, and poems. His drawings were excellent, though they leaned on the darker side—skulls, demons, things of that nature. It was easy to feel the anger in the sketches, like his jaw was clenched as he circled the pen round and round, sometimes tearing through the paper. It felt very much like we were peering into the mind of someone haunted by their inner demons.

There were also quite a few strange-looking feline characters, which matched a tattoo on Carrie's forearm. Joss identified the character as the Cheshire cat from *Alice and Wonderland*. Never having seen the movie myself, I asked Joss about the character. According to her, the cat is a mischievous spirit that guides Alice on her journey. As I stared at the cat's black eyes on the page, I couldn't shake this feeling that I had seen the name Cheshire very recently. I just couldn't quite place it.

JOSS: As we were finishing up with the room, I unearthed a shoebox lodged beneath Tuck's guitars and equipment. The box was stuffed with photos, CDs, and other various trinkets. As I dug through it, one photo caught my eye. A polaroid picture of Kiana and Tuck in a sea of partygoers. Tuck was wearing a cutoff shirt and black pants, his long frame towered over the five-foot nothing Kiana, whose arms were wrapped around his skinny waist. And next to it were two tickets to Wonderland. My first thought. *Could Kiana have been at Wonderland on the night of Tuck's disappearance?* Who else had access to Tuck's belongings, and why would there be two ticket stubs? Cal took a picture of the tickets and polaroid with his phone. Then he took out a CD from the box labeled "Training Sessions" and put it in an external hard drive attached to his computer.

CAL: Tuck appeared shirtless on my computer screen. An assortment of traditional tattoos covered every inch of his lanky body. As he waxed a surfboard, Carrie held the shaky video camera. Here's an audio clip from that recording.

CARRIE: This is my brother and trainer, Tuck. And this is my best friend, Kiana.
[KIANA WAVES]
TUCK: Carrie, enough with the videos. Take this shit seriously.
[TUCK TRIES TO PUT HIS HAND OVER THE CAMERA. CARRIE LAUGHS, AVOIDING HIS ATTEMPT TO STOP TAPING]
CARRIE: C'mon. We'll need the footage for the future doc.
[TUCK GETS UP WITH HIS SURFBOARD. HE STARES AT THE CAMERA, ANGRILY]
TUCK: Turn it off, Carrie! I fucking mean it.
CARRIE: Jesus. Lighten up.
TUCK: Do you know why I take this shit so seriously? Because you're the one good thing I'm doing with my life, all-right? You're not going to become a burnout like me. Or take a dollar of our father's money. Do you fucking hear me? You're going to do something amazing

with your life. Starting with the US Open of Surf. Now will you turn this shit off?

CARRIE: When did my brother start doing drugs? Pretty early on. I know how it started. My father was so hard on Tuck. He tried bringing him to yacht clubs and golf outings. Like he was an accessory to his life. But that wasn't Tuck. My father had no intention of ever trying to understand him. And when he didn't conform, my dad took his anger out on him. I remember one night in particular. He and my father got into a heated argument about his future, and my father ripped out the earring gauge from his ear, leaving a bloody trail across the house. My brother rebelled that night by stealing my stepmom's Oxys and Xanax. His addiction only got worse from there.

But he never showed up to a training session high. I was proud of that.

You said Tuck was going to introduce you to someone, a girlfriend? Any idea who it was?

CARRIE: [SHAKES HEAD] No.

Can you tell us more about Tuck's relationship with Kiana?

[CAL SHOWS CARRIE THE PHOTO]

CARRIE: He loved Kiana like a sister. Those two had a special bond. They were artists. When she got screwed over by her manager and dropped from her label, Tuck literally drove down there to storm the castle. No, whoever Tuck was going to introduce me to, she was new. But sadly, no one ever came forward.

Can you tell me about the tattoo on your arm?

CARRIE: [SMILING] When I was a kid, Tuck used to read me Lewis Caroll's, *Alice's Adventures in Wonderland* every night before bed. **[SNICKERS, SHAKES HER HEAD]** It's just a stupid tattoo.

CAL: Emotions welled in Carrie's eyes as she stared at the faded ink on her forearm. Perhaps this was the one memory she wasn't ready to revisit.

After a few hours, Joss and I prepared to leave. But right when I was about to say goodbye, I remembered where I had seen the name Cheshire. It was in the comments of one of Carrie's recent posts.

CARRIE: Honestly, I got hundreds of comments on everything I posted. I stopped reading them when my account went viral.

CAL: Wasting no time, we located the comment from a user named Cheshire89. It was a simple greeting, *Hello Carrie*. But when Carrie saw this, she put her trembling hand to her mouth, mumbling that eighty-nine was the year Tuck was born. When we clicked on the user, there was no profile picture. No posts. But in the bio was a set of coordinates. Joss quickly typed the coordinates into Google Maps.

CARRIE: When I saw the location, I couldn't believe it. It was the warehouse where the Wonderland rave took place. The last place my brother was seen alive.

CAL: Immediately, Joss and I locked eyes. It was time for a trip to Wonderland.

BELLA ALLESANDRA: Despite the circumstances, our first few days on the island were pleasant. We woke up on a beach with our luggage scattered across the sand. In plain view were eleven thatched huts overlooking pristine water. Clearly not the ideal way to be shown to our rooms, but hey, it was paradise. At least there were no masked men with guns or barbed wire fences. Each cabana had a private butler who served us whatever we wanted—top shelf alcohol, fish tacos, anything. They wanted us nice and fed, ripe for the slaughter. And some of these girls were ripe indeed. Like "buzzed off two hard seltzers" ripe. Everyone was desperate to believe we were going to be okay. **[PAUSES, PLAYS WITH NAILS]**

I mean, who would kidnap eleven of the biggest influencers in the world and hold them hostage? After they shot the promo video, things started to change. On the morning of our third day, we heard Kiki shriek from the shoreline. She was the one who found Billy. He was lying face down in the sand, motionless. When we rolled him over, the girls screamed. We knew he was dead. He had a gold blindfold over his eyes and a message painted in blood on his chest.

Message?

They were rules…Well, more like caveats. We must remain on the beach. We must post three times a day promoting the contest. And lastly, one influencer would be eliminated each day. The one with the lowest engagement. **[SNICKERS]**

The girls did their best to brush the whole thing off. As if Billy did something to deserve being murdered. Yes, he was an asshole. But c'mon? I remember Angel Asher losing her shit on everyone. She yelled, "Are you guys really that dumb? He's going to fucking kill us all."

I liked Angel. She had street smarts. She didn't grow up in country clubs and private schools like the rest of these girls. You can tell when you meet someone who's gone through shit, you know? There's an edge to them. Both Angel and I had that edge. It made us stronger than the others. We built our careers from the ground up, self-made. We were determined to make it off this island alive.

When did the rest of the girls take the threat seriously?

When they took Emily Chavez in the dead of night. I'll never forget that shrill scream. Blood curdling. Like she was ripped from her bed by a monster. When we flipped on the lights of her hut, she was gone. Vanished into the night.

Did Emily have the lowest engagement?

Her content wasn't great, but she wasn't the lowest. But there were rumors. Some of the girls said that Emily's followers were fake. That's one thing you'll learn about Wyatt. He seems to have an aversion to anything that's not authentic. He's a bit of a buzzkill.

Where did they take her?

Wasn't that the million-dollar question? I was the only one brave enough to find out.

JOSS: As soon as we returned from Carrie's apartment, I scheduled an emergency meeting with the team. We were supposed to play the first episode for Eric in less than twenty-four hours, and we needed to pull an all-nighter. The episode was shit, and we all knew it. I did my best to set up the competition and the viral craze sweeping the nation, but there wasn't enough substance. Then there was that giant elephant in the room. What happens if Carrie and Kiana don't get selected? Then what did we have? All this work would be flushed down the toilet. The plan was to ask Eric for an extension. Enough time to at least schedule a trip to the Wonderland warehouse with Carrie. Not to mention getting to the bottom of the Wonderland tickets we found in Tuck's room. We needed to ask Kiana about her whereabouts on the night of Tuck's disappearance.

So we're right in the middle of planning our pitch to Eric, when Cal gets up and just walks out of the room. He said he had somewhere to be.

CAL: I'm not making excuses for how I handled things. I was emotional. But I'll explain. During the meeting, the director of *Yellow Sub,* Lucas Yuvani, sent me a text saying that he was available to meet. This wasn't *just* the director of the show, which Wyatt was potentially a part of. This was a guy whose head was placed on a metal spike in one of Wyatt's most recent digital paintings. If anyone was going to have answers, it was him. He agreed to meet me if I could be in Burbank in forty-five minutes.

JOSS: I don't care what his excuse was. Cal wasn't thinking clearly.

CAL: Yuvani gave me directions to an old diner across the street from the Warner Brothers studio—a Jewish deli with big red leather booths and oversized menus. I spotted him coming through the door. Yuvani was a big man, with receding black hair and a thick, grizzled beard. He sported a loose-fitting polo shirt and tight jogger sweatpants. From the moment he sat down, Yuvani was unsettled, fidgeting with the laminated menu, tapping his designer tennis shoes against the tiles. Amongst stacking ceramic plates and restaurant chatter, I recorded the conversation.

Can you tell me a little about **Yellow Sub?**

YUVANI: It was a good show. One of the few shows I actually enjoyed making. Like it was actual art, you know? Not like the typical network shit I film day in and day out.

Why was it canceled?

YUVANI: You know these fucking networks. It's a numbers game. They throw something against the wall, see if it sticks. If it does, they order more episodes. If not, everyone gets fired and moves on.

Did you know about the painting on the backlot? Did anyone have beef with Paul Riley?

YUVANI: A lot of people had a beef with Riley. Talent never likes the suits that write their paychecks.

What about you? You were the subject of Wyatt's recent art piece. He put your head on a spike.

YUVANI: I'd rather be in a painting than be dead.

What are you talking about?

YUVANI: Listen, I took this meeting to warn you.

[HE LEANS IN, GLANCING SUSPICIOUSLY AROUND THE DINER] Did you know that in the past five years, two people involved with that show have been killed? An assistant producer and an executive producer. Out of respect, I went to those funerals. The family wouldn't say much, but I heard things. **[PAUSES, LEANS CLOSER]**

Things about the bodies.

[WHISPERS]

Their eyes were removed.

Their eyes?

YUVANI: Yes. Whoever killed them, removed the eyes from their fucking sockets.

CAL: What did the police say?

YUVANI: Unsolved. So if I were you, I'd stop asking questions. Drop the story before someone else dies. Don't poke the fucking dragon.

CAL: Then Yuvani drained the last of his coffee, got up, and left.

EPISODE FOUR:

THE SELECTION

CAL: On September 16th, Wyatt James broadcast this message on his website.

AUDIO FROM WYATT JAMES WEBSITE: Thank you for your interest in Influencer Island. Your submissions have been reviewed. In two days, ten souls will be chosen to enter paradise for a transformative experience. May fame and followers be upon you. A word of caution to those digging up secrets. Are you truly prepared to face the answers that you seek? You have been warned.

JOSS: Did I know Wyatt James was speaking directly to Cal? Absolutely not. But on the far chance that he was, I decided that enough was enough. It was time for Cal to come clean about his obsession with James. It was time he let me into his investigation.

CAL: That night when I got home from my meeting with Yuvani, Joss's car was parked outside.

JOSS: As I waited outside Cal's enormous house, I realized how little I knew about him, even though I had been working side by side with him for over three years. Cal was a hard worker. He grinded fourteen-hour days, sometimes sleeping at the office. His entire life was his job. He never talked about his parents, or whether he had siblings, or any family and friends. I knew he'd gone to art school, that he used to paint, but that was about it.

CAL: Joss was the first person from work to see my home, a four-bedroom house in Brentwood that I lived in by myself.

JOSS: The place was cold, filled with dusty, outdated furniture. It smelled like moldy carpet and overflowing ashtrays. Knowing his salary, I assumed it was an inheritance. Cal got me a beer, and we sat down on a velvet sofa in the living room. Immediately, my eyes were drawn to a painting on the wall, a stunning portrait of a young woman, her face fragmented into tiny pieces on the canvas with vines and irises layered over her eyes.

As a seasoned podcaster, Cal turned on the microphone and started recording. He was about to confess everything.

CAL: This was my mother's house. She died of lung cancer a year and a half ago.

JOSS: Sorry, I didn't know.

CAL: My father's name was Isaias Everett.

JOSS: The painter?

CAL: He was famous in the eighties and nineties, known mostly for his abstract portraits, always leaving the eyes unfocused or unseen. My mom said he suffered from a mental illness that left him scattered and often wandering the streets for days on end. But he refused medication. He told doctors that the pills numbed his mind and distorted his art. He believed that his mental suffering was for the greater good.

My mother was always straight with me. She'd met my father when she was nineteen years old, living in Chinatown in San Francisco. One night, she looked out the window and saw this handsome man standing in the middle of the street, spinning around as he stared off into oblivion. My mom went out and asked if he was okay. Isaias said he was looking for inspiration, his next subject to paint. That's the painting you see on the wall.

JOSS: It's beautiful. She was beautiful.

CAL: Thanks. **[TAKES SIP OF BEER]** He stayed in San Francisco for a month, and then—as he did frequently—he vanished into thin air. Over the years, my mom tried to get in contact with him, but he never stayed anywhere long enough. But he took care of us. He bought my mother this house and paid my college tuition. The money was always wired from his agent, who sold my father's paintings and gave him money whenever he reached out.

JOSS: Did you ever meet him?

CAL: No. There was no permanent address. Letters always came back. Phone numbers disconnected. **[PAUSES]** The first time I saw my father in person was at a Wyatt James art exhibition. Suspended in formaldehyde, a gold blindfold over his face, his body mangled and crushed. Around him, eleven portraits made by Wyatt himself. Critics say that they were some of Wyatt's greatest works, that my father must have been Wyatt's muse. What angered me the most wasn't just that he'd exploited my father for his own gain, nor that he put his dead body on display for the world to see. It was that he robbed me of a chance to meet my father. A chance to truly understand where I came from, who I am.

JOSS: Do you think Wyatt killed your father?

CAL: [CLICKS ON COMPUTER] After the installation, Wyatt posted this sound clip along with the pictures of my father on his website.

AUDIO CLIP OF WYATT JAMES: I shall never wash the blood from my hands. My tribute to a fallen genius.

JOSS: That's not quite a confession.

CAL: It sounds like a man who was jealous of my father. I know Wyatt had something to do with Isaias's death. Or at least he knows how he died. The truth must come out. He needs to be brought to justice. I need to know what happened to him.

JOSS: As a friend, I wanted to support Cal. As his coworker, as his *assistant producer*, I should have been straight with him. I enabled him. But I've always had a soft spot for Cal.

CAL: That night, Joss sat down and helped me organize the investigation.

JOSS: First, we smoked a joint and watched the only three episodes of *Yellow Sub* in existence. The show was good. The cast was incredible. We had Janet, the quirky, hilarious mom and lead singer. Jack, the guitar player and more down-to-earth realist. And Mandy, their adorable and inquisitive child.

CAL: After our stoned binge-watch, Joss told me she had a surprise.

JOSS: Cal hadn't known, but once I realized what he was doing, I opened his little Wyatt James obsession box he'd left at the office. I have to admit, there was some interesting stuff in there.

CAL: One thing I could never crack was Wyatt World, a dark web forum protected with heavy tech. Three failed attempts and they blocked your VPN and IP from the login page.

JOSS: Cal is a good producer, but he's an average journalist. Within hours of searching, I had a contact who got me the password.

CAL: Christmas morning came early.

JOSS: As soon as we logged in, there was a landing page with Wyatt's masked face. Beneath that was a strange disclaimer, written in a pixelated font. I copied it down so we could read it word for word:

Welcome to the dark world of Wyatt James. Our leader illuminates the false Gods that live amongst us. Poisoning the minds of idle sheep. If you do not wish to support Wyatt's mission in burning this toxic civilization to the ground, exit at once. If you leak or share anything from Wyatt World, we will find you.

CAL: Wyatt World was a conspiracy theorist's paradise. There was talk of strange symbols and secret cults. How the government is exploiting celebrities to distract us from their real objectives. Evidently, there's an experimental lab with secret bunkers and dungeons beneath the Getty Museum. Or did you know there's a hidden chamber beneath the Hollywood sign where tech titans and Hollywood elite meet to discuss world domination? I didn't.

But there were also other things. Things that *did* interest me. Things that pulled me deeper down the rabbit hole. Unseen Wyatt James paintings from the last few years. Portraits of serial killers from all over the world. Drug lords from Eastern Europe. Even a peculiar audio clip from an unaired interview he did for an underground Hungarian radio station.

AUDIO CLIP FROM WYATT JAMES: My father was my first subject. A broken valve at a chemical plant and a flurry of steam disintegrated his eyes. To paint his soul, I looked to other places. His swollen cheeks. His furrowed brow. His twisted smile. To the creases on his skin. Evidence of the darkness dwelling within. I found truth in the subtleties. I found meaning in them. Now I only paint portraits with the subject's eyes obscured.

JOSS: Who knew if that audio recording was real or not. Wyatt World was a shithole, a cesspool of misinformation. If it wasn't for me, Cal would have ingested that crap until the sun came up. Luckily, I spotted a thread entitled "Mission Yellow Sub." It turns out that Cal wasn't the first one to make the connection between Wyatt and the canceled sitcom. There were at least thirty users who'd discovered the leaked promo art and the distinctive blur across the eyes. And there was so much more. Someone in Wyatt World uncovered an internal investigation from Warner Brothers. They had camera footage.

CAL: Watching the real Wyatt James paint on the studio wall was a surreal experience. You couldn't see his face, of course. He wore black pants and a black hoodie, black ski-mask to match. Plus, the security camera didn't have the best angle. But as I watched him paint, I felt rage swirl in my veins. My anger ran deep.

JOSS: But that's not all the internal investigation dug up. It turned out there was a suspect.

CAL: In an internal memo, security reported that Ian Huckle, the actor who'd played the husband on *Yellow Sub*, drove up to the studio gate the day the show was canceled. According to the front gate attendant, Ian launched into a drunken tirade after finding out his credentials had been revoked. That was when he turned to the security camera and screamed for Paul Riley to come out and face him like a man. Before police arrived, Ian left on his own accord, screaming, "Tell Riley I'll be back!"

JOSS: It turned out Ian Huckle had a string of documented attacks against Riley. Several lewd comments were screenshotted from a deleted Twitter account, in which Ian called Riley a chauvinistic pig, and that he would get what was coming to him.

Then there was the fact that Ian had vacated Hollywood after the pilot was canceled. This was no small thing, since Huckle had been a working actor since his twenties. According to Wyatt World, Ian deleted his social media accounts when the show ended. In fact, there wasn't a single record of him again until 2015, around the same time of the first DIED FAMOUS installment, when he rented a small commercial unit in La Brea under the LLC name, Yellow Cat Imports. The address was unlisted, but the forum had a wide range of abandoned buildings and locations that users believed could be Wyatt's secret studio.

JOSS: Then Cal opened the browser to a casting headshot of Ian Huckle, which was posted on Wyatt World with the caption "The Real Wyatt James." Ian was a handsome guy. Rugged, mid-thirties, strong jawline. Cal couldn't stop staring at the picture, as if he was trying to ascertain whether or not he was really staring at the face of his father's killer. There was almost a look of dissatisfaction and remorse on Cal's face. This wasn't the way he wanted to find out.

CAL: This obsession haunted me for years. Where would I be without it? But the proof was in the thread. The evidence was substantial.

BELLA ALLESANDRA: After Emily was kidnapped, we stopped singing kumbaya and braiding each other's hair. You could feel the tension. Some of us thrived on the competition. It made our content better. If Kiki posted a half-naked photo, then I took an even thirstier photo.

I formed an alliance with the girls who had over 10 million followers. We called our little pod The BFIs, The Big Fucking Influencers. **[LAUGHING]** It was me, Angel Asher, Kiki Kelly, Sienna Owens, and my friend Olivia Ray. We were the strongest of the bunch. We all slept in the same cabana, each of us taking turns on watch. Every night a piercing scream rang out from somewhere in the camp. And each morning, we'd find another girl missing. From eleven down to five.

They came for Olivia on our final night at the cabanas. Kiki was supposed to be on watch. **[PAUSES, SHAKES HER HEAD]**

Olivia was sleeping right next to me. I felt her hand latch onto my wrist. Someone covered her mouth to smother her scream. I reached for her arm, but she was being dragged through the door by masked men into the darkness. The sound of her acrylics clawing into the wooden floorboards still haunts me. The other girls woke up, looking around like a bunch of helpless idiots. I couldn't just stand back and watch. I wasn't raised to be a coward. I followed her screams into the jungle.

CAL: As the influencers were being snatched up on the island, users on Reddit began connecting the dots.

LANE: Despite what the FBI claims, the Redditors were the first to discover the larger conspiracy at play. There was a thread on the site called *Dead Influencers*. In it, a user named SuperSkull3 was the first to post screenshots from an exclusive underground auction house known as DARK WATERS. Wyatt James was auctioning new digital portraits, starting with Billy Atlas and Emily Chavez. In traditional Wyatt James fashion, the influencer portraits had a golden line over the subject's eyes. But there was also something very untraditional about the paintings. In the description, it stated that the digital images would transform eleven days after Influencer Island concluded. So people who bought the damn thing had no idea what it was going to turn into.

Did that matter?

Not in the slightest. The first portrait of Emily sold for two million dollars. The rest sold for much more than that.

CAL: In the thread, the Redditors tracked the activities of every influencer on the island. Their evidence was convincing: Each time an influencer portrait went up for auction on DARK

WATERS, that person stopped posting new content. They weren't seen in photos. They just disappeared. The theory was simple: Wyatt James was killing off influencers one by one. The world was just too blind or too stupid to notice.

CAL: On the day the contestants were supposed to be announced, my team scheduled a trip with Carrie to the old *Los Angeles Times* printing factory in Orange County.

This was the site of Wonderland, a rave hosted by renowned DJ Mad DoX, famous for wearing an outlandish Mad Hatter-style hat while he performs. This was Tuck's final destination before he was declared missing.

According to reports dug up by our team, Mad DoX, real name Edward Dockins, set up 90+ cameras in the old factory that night, which he planned on using for an upcoming music video. There was just one problem. Within hours of the rave ending, most of the footage was stolen and deleted from the musician's hard drive. Someone was hiding something.

Carrie met us in the factory's abandoned parking lot at 3:00 p.m. The plan was simple. The team would follow Carrie inside. We'd keep the cameras and audio rolling the entire time. But right when we were all set up and ready to enter, Carrie received a message. Judging by the way she held her breath, I knew it was something serious.

CARRIE: It was a direct message from Cheshire89. Whoever it was, they requested that I enter the warehouse alone. Imagine some unknown person using your brother's nickname to leave cryptic messages on your account, then asking you to revisit the place he was last seen. I had no idea what I was going to find inside that factory.

BELLA ALLESANDRA: I followed Olivia's screams through the jungle for hours. I'm not some stick figure model. I ran track in high school. But these guys—whoever kidnapped her—was a supernatural demon. One minute she's there, and the next she's gone. But I kept running, deeper and deeper into the thick jungle. Until I was staggering through the trees. I don't know what I was looking for. Help. Death. Anything was better than going back to the camp and waiting. After hours of wandering, I came across this sliver of smoke rising over the treetops. At the tree line, I witnessed the source of the smoke. A giant fire blazing on the beach. That was when I spotted Olivia. This time, it was *my* scream that needed to be stifled.

CAL: Carrie shook as we mic'd her up in the parking lot. I reassured her that our team wasn't going anywhere. We'd be right here, listening to the recording. If we sensed any danger, we'd come in straight away. I told her to narrate everything going on. It would be like we were right by her side. Carrie nodded, then stared at the abandoned warehouse with her steely blue, unwavering eyes. She was tougher than we gave her credit for. No matter what ended up happening, I admired that about her.

AUDIO FROM CARRIE'S MIC: Alright, so I'm stepping through the door. It smells like shit in here. All sorts of corroded equipment. Water dripping from the ceiling. Giant puddles and heaps of trash. A bunch of rusted staircases that lead to the second level. Just looks like an abandoned factory to me. Not sure what I'm looking for. Wait, I hear something. It sounds like a voice. Do you hear that?

CAL: Out of nowhere, the mic let out a high-pitched frequency, followed by static. Our signal was shot.

Did you freak out when Carrie went offline?

No. I kept a level head.

JOSS: Please. He *totally* freaked out. Knight in shining armor was ready to gallop in on his white horse. But I talked him down. She was instructed to go in alone.

CARRIE: I trailed the voice deeper into the factory, trying to find the source. It was him, Wyatt James. You can't mistake his demonic voice. It was some sort of welcome message. Like, *Thank you for your interest in Influencer Island. Please continue to the main viewing hall.*

Finally, I found the source of the recording. It was coming from an enormous concrete room, the length of a football field, completely cleared out, except for rubble scattered across the floor. On one of the walls was a projector playing video clips from the night of Wonderland. One of them immediately caught my attention. There was no mistaking my brother walking through a metal door. Then I saw a different video. Another person in a black hoodie walking through the same door.

JOSS: Unexpectedly, while we were sitting there waiting for Carrie, I received a message from one of my contacts. He found the address for Ian Huckle's business, Yellow Cat Imports. When I plugged it into my phone, I located a rundown commercial building, only twenty minutes North. I was about to show Cal when everyone's phones buzzed with notifications.

CAL: Wyatt James went live an hour earlier than expected. The contestants were about to be announced. The only thing in the frame were ten blank canvases. I speculated that it was coming from the abandoned factory. But after closer inspection, I noticed that the room was much smaller, some kind of basement. So when Joss showed me the address of Ian Huckle's business, I was convinced we found him. This was where Ian Huckle was livestreaming the selection.

Joss can say whatever she wants about my feelings for Carrie. My desire for vengeance outweighed everything. I told Amy and Tony to wait for Carrie to make contact. I was going North to expose Wyatt James.

BELLA ALLESANDRA: When I got to the beach, a giant bonfire with twenty-foot flames came into view. Standing around those flames were dozens of men with ski masks, chanting in some foreign language. It was some dark shit. And in the midst of all of them was Olivia, tied to a chair, perched behind a blank canvas. The poor girl was barely alive. Her face was pale as a ghost with sweat and blood dripping down her forehead. I was about to run toward her, when I stopped dead in my tracks. Because there he was, Wyatt James, stepping into the firelight, sitting down behind the canvas. Then he started painting.

CAL: It took us twenty minutes to get to Ian's commercial space. The industrial park was a cluster of units with rolling white sheet doors. It was the perfect hiding place for a secret studio. The front door was locked but the rolling door was open.

JOSS: The place was trashed. Boxes emptied. Desks overturned. Hundreds of papers strewn across the cheap blue carpet. Someone had already raided the place.

CAL: Joss and I split up, rummaging through the office. In one of the deserted rooms, I found a box full of photos dumped out. The only one I recognized was a picture of the entire *Yellow Sub* cast. Three of the people in the picture had X's crossed out over their faces. One of them was Ian Huckle. I assumed the others were the deceased members associated with the show. When I flipped to the next picture, I recoiled in shock. It was a charcoal sketch of Ian Huckle, a blurred streak covering his eyes. As I stared deeply at the sketch, I heard Joss scream.

CARRIE: There were so many questions running through my head as I stared at those videos of Tuck at Wonderland. Were those the last moments of my brother's life? Was the man in the black hoodie responsible for his disappearance? Why was Wyatt James showing me this? Then suddenly, the projector stopped. Instinctively, I knew where Wyatt was directing me. I went to the next room, deeper into the factory. My gaze fell straight to the metal door that Tuck had walked through. But now, it was stenciled with the Influencer Island logo, a social media-like icon with a skull and the number ten.

CAL: I sprinted through the office, yelling Joss's name. I found her on the far side of the garage, amongst a sea of boxes and metal shelving. She was standing there, shaking, her hands covering her mouth. She pointed to something in the middle of the room: a man tied to a chair. The actor known as Ian Huckle.

CARRIE: I walked through the door, into this abandoned concrete room. And I know this sounds crazy, but I could feel Tuck's energy. I could sense his presence in that room. On the wall, the phrase, "Down the Rabbit Hole," was spray painted on cement.

Did that mean something to you?

Of course. It was an *Alice's Adventures in Wonderland* reference. But quite literally, the phrase was referencing a hole in the concrete floor. There was a metal ladder that led to the basement. I followed the instructions into the darkness. All I could hear was the sound of water dripping from the ceiling. I turned on my phone's flashlight, tiptoeing through the murky basement. Finally, I saw a flickering light at the far end of the room. When I got close enough, the silhouette of a man tied to a chair came into view. My heart pounded in my chest as his face became visible. I couldn't believe what I was seeing. I thought my mind was playing tricks on me. It was my brother, Tuck.

BELLA ALLESANDRA: I knew Wyatt had finished painting Olivia, because the masked men stopped chanting. I was on pins and needles. Only the sound of the flames whipping in the wind was heard. Wyatt stood up, and I watched Olivia's head roll to the side. That's when I saw her eyes. They were dark as night. Like she was possessed by the fucking devil. My scream came out of nowhere. I tried to cover it up, but it was too late. The masked men turned and spotted me.

CAL: I instantly started gagging. Ian Huckle was slumped over in a chair, ropes tied across his chest, blood dripping from a thin gash in his neck. But that's not what made me sick. It was the flies buzzing around his empty eye sockets. We didn't have to check his pulse. He was dead.

CARRIE: Seeing my brother in that basement... I just had this overwhelming sense of relief. He was alive. I wasn't crazy for not losing hope. And with him back—everything was going to be okay. I was going to be okay. I didn't need this competition. I didn't need anything. I had my brother back. Tuck was the only thing I ever truly cared about in this life. **[WIPES TEAR]**

But when I got close enough to touch him, I noticed that his image was fading in and out, glitching. It was a hologram. One of the first of Wyatt's many mindfucks. I was on my knees, crying, screaming in frustration, when this flood of bright light washed over me. Then dramatic music blared through the basement, this pulsing drum that pounded through the small space.

LANE: With over ten million people tuned into this Livestream, Wyatt came out onto the screen and spray-painted the username of each contestant on a blank canvas. Then the video cut to the contestants, live from the spot their invitations (the 'II' logo) were discovered. The invitations were spray-painted in ten locations across the globe, from a cave in Kentucky to the side of a Gucci store in London. None of the contestants spoke. They just appeared live on screen while that eerie cinematic contest theme song played. Carrie and Kiana were the final two selected. Both looked like they had seen a ghost.

CARRIE: Imagine if you thought you had the most important person in your life back, only to have them taken away again. How would you react?

KIANA AUDIO FROM RADIO INTERVIEW: My invitation was on a lifeguard tower that had a lot of history for me. I don't know how, but Wyatt knew our darkest secrets and deepest fears.

BELLA ALLESANDRA: Wyatt's goons chased me through the jungle. I was running for my life, weaving in and out of the palm trees, desperate not to share the same fate as Olivia. Finally, I spotted a cave to take refuge in. If I just survived until daylight.

I must have sat in the darkness for hours, rocking back and forth in the cold, praying that I had shaken them off. At some point in the night, I was jolted awake by torchlight burning in the cavern. Wyatt James emerged from the darkness, his masked goons by his side. Then my friends were brought forth, thrown to the ground like ragdolls. Kiki, Sienna, and Angel. All of them were on their knees, blindfolded, shaking in their boots. **[PAUSES, SNICKERS]**

I thought they were going to line us up and shoot us one by one. Instead, Wyatt circled around us with torch in hand. Then he finished the story of King James. He said: When the greedy sailors awoke after the feast, they found themselves tied to wooden planks next to a roaring fire on the beach. Then King James would give the captives two choices. Either renounce their identity and become his disciples or be burned alive. Most sailors had to be inserted into the flames before they took the first option. According to James, the sailors emerged from the flames disfigured and faceless, but more importantly, they were purified, ready to embrace their new purpose.

So what happened?

I yelled, "Then do it. Get this over with."

Wyatt just smiled behind the torchlight. He said our jobs were not yet finished. He said we have proven to be the strongest of the group. That we shall become his contest ambassadors.

So you accepted?

As if we had a choice. Right before Wyatt left, he glanced around the cave and said, "Would you like to know what happened to those who refused to submit?" Then he shined the light across the cavern, illuminating thousands of skulls set into the stone.

You seriously have no idea how delusional this man was. How dangerous he was. The terror we dealt with.

Even if you find these girls, there will be nothing left of them. Don't you see? He ripped out their souls and sold them off to the highest bidder. He didn't just kill them. That would be too easy. He dug up their demons and then broke them into a million pieces.

CAL: When the cops arrived at the Yellow Cat space to take statements, Joss and I were in shock. We were staring at our phones, trying to process everything. All bets were off. Now that

Carrie and Kiana were chosen, the real work was beginning. For better or worse, we would chase Wyatt James all the way until the bitter end.

CARRIE: Listen, if you want me to tell you if I thought my brother was dead or alive, the answer is alive. If you want me to tell you that I knew Wyatt James was going to lead me to the truth, no, I didn't know shit. I didn't know what awaited me on that island. I didn't know how fucked up things were going to get.

[PART 2]

MEET THE CONTESTANTS

EPISODE FIVE:

THE CONTESTANTS

CAL: Twenty-four hours into Agent Michelle Cooper's investigation on Devil's Cay, and there was very little good news to relay back to Washington. Moreover, Agent Cooper and her team were starting to feel the effects of the island.

AGENT COOPER: There was something so eerie about Devil's Cay, something you couldn't quite shake. Other agents expressed similar sentiments. It was like this malignant shadow that settled over us, the way fog settles over the bay. From sundown to sunup, you could hear this spine-chilling hissing sound of the poisonous snakes that overran the jungle.

We searched that island high and low for survivors. It was one dead contestant after the next. A contestant with her face completely mashed in. Another crucified to a palm tree. But nothing compares to the massacre down at East Beach—seven mutilated bodies arranged into an X. Well, what was left of their bodies anyway. Most of them had missing legs, arms, and of course, no eyes. The things we saw on that island... It sticks with you.

How was the investigation into the missing influencers going?

Not good. Nine of the original influencers and one contestant were still unaccounted for. We were all aware of the pressure we were under. We turned Wyatt's abandoned camp into a command center. Day and night, my team interviewed the survivors, trying to get information that could lead us to the others. **[TAKES SIP OF COFFEE]** And then we got the tip about Kiana Martin. Her testimony was the key to finding the missing influencers.

CAL: The FBI found Kiana Martin ten days after the competition. In a photo that went viral, the talented singer was seen wandering the streets of Havana with a buzzed haircut, dirty gray sweatpants, and a ragged hoodie. According to Agent Cooper, when the FBI apprehended her, she did not respond to her name.

AGENT COOPER: It took us a while to get her to talk. Kiana looked nothing like the girl we had seen in the media. She had all the signs of having been through some sort of indoctrination or ritualistic initiation. But when she finally sat down to talk, there was a sense of calmness to her, a lightness. It became clear that she was sent to us for a reason.

CAL: What you are about to hear is the FBI's debriefing of Kiana Martin.

[FBI INTERVIEW OF KIANA MARTIN]:

Can you state your name for the record?

KIANA: I have no name. I am nothing. I am…

You are not Kiana Martin, born and raised in Newport Beach, California?

I have no earthly name. I am a disciple of The Eleven.

The Eleven? Is this the cult that Wyatt James was a part of?

[SILENCE]

Can you tell me about this society?

[SILENCE]

Can you tell us where you have been?

I have been purged of my sins.

Do you know where Wyatt James is?

My master does not wish to be found yet.

Why were you released?

I am here to do my part in the Great Awakening. My master and the elders have much planned. I am here to lead you to the next chapter.

Do you know where the others are?

I shall not speak of them. Their duties are not yet complete.

Can you tell me what happened to Kiana Martin then?

[PAUSES, SMILES]

She died on the island with everyone else.

CAL: As we enter this next part of the story, there is another personal detail I must disclose. On the day the contestants were chosen, the same day we found Ian Huckle dead, my relationship with Carrie Andrews changed significantly. That night, I wasn't in a good place. I was second guessing myself. Was I in over my head? Should I quit the podcast, let the police handle it from here on out?

By midnight, I found myself drinking heavily, browsing through a shoebox of my mom's old photos when I came across my favorite picture: My mother and father beaming in an abandoned warehouse in the Dogpatch district of San Francisco. My mother wore a cotton dress with her favorite flower, an iris, tucked behind her ear. She loved my father, despite everything. I never blamed him for not being a part of my life, either. I always empathized with his mental illness. But after Wyatt's installation, that's when the resentment surfaced. I needed answers. I was deep in thought when I heard a knock on the door.

CARRIE: I didn't want to be by myself that night. Seeing that hologram of my brother… **[PAUSES]** It shook me. I would have called Kiana, but we had grown distant. She was consumed with her newfound fame. But for me, I was more alone than ever. I didn't know where I belonged. I didn't have an industry to fit into like her. I wasn't a surfer. I wasn't a model. I wasn't anything.

I took a midnight drive to clear my head and I ended up at… well, you know the rest. You weren't like any of the guys I've ever dated. You're completely awkward. You don't play guitar or surf. You don't have tattoos. But there was something about you. We shared something. A sadness, I guess. Something inside of you that I recognized in myself. Like you understood what I was going through. Something that made me feel less alone. Maybe there's more to it… I don't know. **[SMILES]** Or maybe I knew you had a thing for me, and it was a pity hookup.

CAL: It's funny how intimidated I was by Carrie. I had been watching her online for weeks. This charismatic, totally out-of-my -league woman. And yet, face to face, she was so real and vulnerable. It made me like her even more. For the first time since my mother died, I didn't feel alone. Carrie offered me something I haven't had in a long time: Hope.

That night, I remember rubbing the scar on Carrie's knee, feeling this raw sadness pour out of her. In my head, it was the start of something real. We were lying in bed, and she asked me for a favor. She asked me to find out what happened to her brother on the night he disappeared. I promised her I would do my best. Maybe I should have told her about the pair of Wonderland tickets we found in Tuck's shoebox. But I wanted to have answers first.

JOSS: Did I want to tell the team about Cal and Carrie? Sure. But it wasn't my place. Cal told me it was a one-time thing. They were done. I wanted to believe him. I wanted to make a great podcast.

CARRIE: The next morning, I took an Uber home from Cal's place. It was gloomy that day, the ocean was cold and gray, and I had this desire to feel the water on my skin. I took off my sandals and I waded into the choppy waves until the water was up to my waist. I closed my eyes and ran my palms on the surface of the water. That was the first surfing lesson Tuck ever taught me. He told me that waves gave off vibrations. This kinetic energy that you have to connect with. **[PAUSES]** That morning was the first time back in the ocean since Tuck went missing. I felt him that morning. And I remember being so mad, just screaming at the sky, screaming at him. FUCK YOU. FUCK YOU FOR LEAVING ME! **[SNICKERS]** I must have looked like such a crazy person. I was holding onto so much anger.

Why?

So many reasons. For giving up on me. For disappearing. For taking the one thing I love [surfing] away from me.

Can you tell me why you quit?

It started with the accident. I'm reminded of it every time I see that ugly scar on my knee. I'd gotten tumbled before, hundreds of times. But the waves in Half Moon Bay were merciless, all powerful. I should have never been in those waves. I felt my knee snap on the first wave that crashed down. But that was just the beginning. The ocean grabbed hold and buried me under its cold depths, pummeling me over and over, until I gave up hope of escaping. I stopped fighting. It was my brother who pulled me out on his jet ski, dragging my limp body back to the shore. By the time I made it to the sand, I was screaming, crying, holding my knee in pain. It was the first time I genuinely saw Tuck scared. He knew how bad it was. It was his fault for bringing me into those waves, and he knew the horrible path to recovery ahead. How hard it would be for me to surf again, let alone compete. But that wasn't the day I quit surfing. That would come later…

CAL: Meanwhile back on the island, the four remaining influencers had become Wyatt's contest ambassadors.

BELLA ALLESANDRA: It was classic cult bullshit. Build you up so they can break you down again. The four of us were taken back to Wyatt's coastal camp and provided a lavish tent, equipped with canopied beds, a full closet of clothes, even a tub the size of a car. But despite the amenities, there was no rest. I know they were putting something in our food. Or maybe it was just the energy in that god damn place. I had this recurring nightmare where I was being buried alive by rotting corpses. They were holding me down and trying to claw my eyes out. I woke up that first morning screaming with Sienna comforting me in bed. She kept trying to tell me that the worst was over. That we survived. That it was all okay now. **[SCOFFS]** I guess it was nice believing the lie.

We spent the next few days roaming around the camp, drinking expensive champagne and lounging in sun chairs while the masked men went about their business. A few times, after six or seven glasses of champagne, I saw Kiki staring over the side of the cliff, wondering if she would survive the fall. She knew death would have been better than what came next.

Did you ever investigate the camp?

There was a lot of movement. We knew they were planning something big. One afternoon, after a few drinks, I decided to wander into one of the lackey's tents. When I peeled open the flap, I saw a masked man staring at himself in the mirror. When he pulled off his ski mask, I recoiled in shock. It wasn't a man. It was a young woman with hideous burns on her face. I'll never forget her creepy smile, staring at me in the reflection. **[PAUSES]** Let's just say I stopped roaming after that.

CARRIE: When I returned home from my little swim, a limo was waiting for me in front of my apartment. The driver told me to make myself presentable—that I was going before Wyatt James. **[LAUGHS]** As if I was meeting royalty. I'll admit, I was nervous. It took me thirty minutes to find the right outfit. I chose ripped black jeans and my brother's old Grateful Dead t-shirt.

As we drove, I assessed the outcome of selection night. My follower count had reached a million. I was getting messages from all sorts of verified celebrities congratulating me on my success. As if I did anything to earn those followers. I stalked the rest of the competition on the drive. There was a pair of gorgeous six-foot model sisters from London, Thalia and Tia. A pretty blonde, redneck hunter from Kentucky. A video game streamer from France. A steroidal neanderthal from Jersey. A hipster photographer from LA and a party couple from Vegas rounded out the group.

The limo finally pulled up to a random block on Hollywood Boulevard, in front of a seedy abandoned storefront with blacked-out windows. When the limo opened, two men with ski masks escorted me out of the car and into the empty store. All the contestants were huddled together on scuffed black and white tiles in the middle of the room. My gaze went straight to Kiana. I was so relieved to see my best friend. From her puffy eyes and disheveled hair, I knew she went through something on selection night. When we hugged, her arms wrapped tightly around me. I didn't need her to apologize for being MIA. I didn't blame her. She was using the opportunity to get back what she lost. In some ways, I think she was relieved to be free of me. I held her back after I lost Tuck. I know that. I was drowning in my own bullshit. But I was so thankful we were going to the island together.

For the next hour, we sat around trying to figure out what Wyatt had in store for us.

The Jersey meathead, Trevor, thought it was going to be a survivor man scenario. The London models thought it was going to be one big party. But the techy French girl, Andrea, was the closest. She had been following all the Reddit threads. "It's going to be a game," she said, "a game where Wyatt exploits our greatest fears and pits us against each other."

I'll never forget the way that hillbilly, Nicki Mo, stared at me. The way her dark blue eyes narrowed on me like an injured deer she wanted to skin and eat on the spot. Then Andrea pulled out her phone from her baggy jeans. "And I'm going to document the whole thing." She turned on her live feed just in time for the big announcement over a cheap speaker dangling from the ceiling.

AUDIO OF WYATT JAMES FROM ANDREA'S ACCOUNT:
Welcome contestants. Each of you have received an invitation to Influencer Island, which has been placed on your phone. There are only ten invitations in existence. You have two options. Leave this room and sell your invitation to the highest bidder, which as of right now, is ten million dollars. Or you destroy it and accept your summons. In the next week, I will make you larger than life, and you will become greater than the influencers and celebrities you admire. But there is a catch. The island will be a transformative experience

that will either grant you enlightenment or
bring you death. The choice is up to you.

CARRIE: As soon as his speech was over, two masked men came out of a curtained room in the back. Everyone had the same bewildered face: Like holy shit, what is this? This wasn't a reality show you watch on *Bravo*. But then there was the *other* thing. Larger than life. Legends. Bigger than the influencers you admire. I could almost feel everyone's excitement bursting out of them. When I glanced down on my phone display, there was an unrecognizable app installed. When I clicked it, the 'II' logo appeared, the social media heart icon with a skull and number. I was invitation number ten.

CAL: Here's the audio from Andrea's live feed.

AUDIO FROM ANDREA'S ACCOUNT:
GRAHAM [PHOTOGRAPHER FROM LOS ANGELES]: Ten
million dollars. That's a lot of money.
THALIA [MODEL FROM LONDON]: But imagine how
much we'll make when we're famous?
TREVOR [TRAINER FROM NEW JERSEY]: More than
famous. He said he'll make us legends.
ANDREA [STREAMER FROM FRANCE]: If we survive.
This isn't going to be a vacation.
DAN [PROMOTER FROM VEGAS]: Can't be worse than
the shit we see in Vegas.
DANIELLE [PROMOTER FROM VEGAS]: Baby, I don't
know about this.
TREVOR: Fuck it. I like my chances. How do I
destroy this thing?
ANDREA: You have to burn it.
TREVOR: Anyone have a lighter?
ANDREA: Not literally. It's how you destroy
something digital.

TREVOR: I don't speak fucking nerd. Just help me do it.

CARRIE: Andrea grabbed Trevor's phone, and with a few clicks, she handed it back. The deed was done. The masked guards grabbed his muscly arms and led him into the back of the store, leaving us in silence. Then I turned to Kiana. Her decision was written on her face. She wasn't going back to her old life. I guess we all felt the same. **[SHAKES HEAD]** The couple from Vegas [Dan and Danielle] debated back and forth for a bit. But in the end, not a single one of us turned down our invites. We all got what was coming to us.

One by one, the masked men led us down a long spiral staircase, at least a hundred feet beneath the floor. The destination was an old prohibition bar beneath the city. But it had been converted into a creepy art studio. There were broken frames and splattered paint everywhere. A wall of wax human and animal heads, and disturbing portraits of celebrities with their faces scratched out. And there was some sort of symbol.

Did it look like this?

[SHOWS XIIX symbol]

Yeah, it was painted all over the room. But they didn't give us time to wander about. Our destination was clear—ten chairs had been placed on a white sheet with canvases. The same canvases that Wyatt painted for selection night. We were told to sit down in front of our names and wait. We must have sat there for an hour. Then the sound of stomping boots echoed on the metal stairs. There was something so awe-inspiring, so powerful about Wyatt James. His presence sent chills down my body. Almost like I craved his attention. Like I wanted him to notice me. Then he sat in front of Thalia, behind her canvas and he asked one question – *What do you want from this experience?*

CAL: Andrea's feed was dark, but it caught the audio of everyone's responses.

THALIA: I want to be a supermodel.
TIA: I want to be on the cover of Vogue.
ANDREA: I want to disrupt culture.
GRAHAM: I want to be a celebrity artist like you.
NICKI MO: I want to hunt a creature worthy of my skills.
TREVOR: I want to be a fucking legend.
DAN: I want to be part of the greatest party in the world.
DANIELLE: I want to be famous.
KIANA: I want the career that was stolen from me.

CARRIE: Then he sat down in front of me. Despite the nerves, I had this desire to look at him. Beyond that dirty ski mask. Through the black netting covering his eyes, I saw the slightest glint of his pupils. There was something so dark, so eerie and broken, but something so familiar. I knew those eyes. And then I looked right at him and said, "I want to know what happened to my brother." He didn't say a word. He just nodded and then stood up. The next time we would see Wyatt was on the island. The circumstances would be much, much, different.

CAL: In the days that followed their selection, the ten contestants became an absolute phenomenon. There were only two weeks before the contest started, and an accelerated press tour commenced. Interviews of each contestant appeared in *Teen Vogue*, *People*, and *Us Weekly*. The front page of *Rolling Stone* and

The Hollywood Reporter. They were on Good Morning America, Live with Kelly and Ryan, and Jimmy Kimmel.

AUDIO CLIP FROM KIMMEL: [APPLAUSE] We have a special episode tonight. All ten contestants from Influencer Island are here. Brave, brave souls, these kids. Going to an unknown island to compete in a contest presided over by someone who paints dead people for a living. That's like a pig entering a competition designed by a butcher. **[LAUGHTER]** "Do it for Gl!tch" is about to take on a whole new meaning. Who's ready to meet the contestants of Influencer Island?

LANE: There were posters and bobble head dolls. Full magazine spreads. My favorite media was probably their *Entertainment Weekly* cover. The headline: "Who's Influencing Your Children?" These kids were everywhere. Literally, it was all anyone talked about at the water cooler.

CAL: As the contestants became larger than life, my boss pushed us to release the first episode of the podcast. He even had the graphics department create marketing materials for the series.

JOSS: His excitement didn't last long. After hearing the first cut, Eric heaved the mockup poster from the easel. He was irate. The podcast was not ready to air. It was full of holes. And after their little night of romance, Cal couldn't get a follow-up with either Kiana or Carrie. **[CHUCKLES]** That's why you don't sleep with your subject.

CAL: After our night together, Carrie wasn't returning my calls. Either she was avoiding me, or her newfound fame kept her busy. I chose to focus on the latter. Since the selection, Carrie's follower count reached a staggering 2.5 million.

JOSS: Even with Kiana and Carrie's early interviews, we needed more meat. There wasn't enough substance to launch a full series, especially since there were no eyes and ears on the island. We needed another angle. Another story to follow.

CAL: That's when Joss had an idea.

JOSS: I suggested we make Cal a secondary subject of the podcast. It made sense. He was in so deep at this point. And this mysterious connection to Wyatt and his father. It was too juicy not to address.

CAL: As you can imagine, I was resistant. I was dealing with stuff I needed to work out on a therapy couch, not on a podcast. But after all the lies and deception, I owed Joss. I owed my team.

JOSS: Cal agreed to visit the Point Arroyo Mental Institute in Burbank. The institution, a cement compound with busted windows and scattered debris, had been vacant for a decade. Three years prior, Wyatt James made the facility into one of his more elaborate DIED FAMOUS installations. Amidst the rubble and rusted remains of the former hospital, Wyatt displayed eleven portraits of Cal's Father, Isaias Everett.

We mic'd up Cal as we entered the building.

The place was still in shambles with sinks and hospital beds strewn across the main entrance. Cal walked into the former cafeteria, the site of Wyatt's exhibit. I asked him if he could recall his experience.

AUDIO FROM INTERVIEW WITH CAL: I remember my heart pounding as I spun around the gallery, staring at the recreations of my father's mind. Eleven portraits of someone who'd battled with inner demons. The Artist. The Patient. The Lover. The Shadow. The Light. And then there was The Father, a portrait with a small smirk twisting in the corner of Isaias's mouth, his eyes obscured by a thin golden bar. It was my least favorite painting. I hated that smirk. It made me think that he considered his role as a father a joke. As if he found my suffering humorous. Did he have any remorse for leaving me?

JOSS: Finally, Cal walked to the spot where Wyatt's final depiction of Isaias stood. It was called The Dead.

CAL: It was one of the worst moments of my life, staring at my father's mangled body, suspended in a sea of formaldehyde. I remember all the other attendees talking loudly amongst themselves, remarking on how innovative the piece was. I stood there in shock, trying to process my father's death. I wanted to know how he died. What his last words were. Did he regret not getting to know me? That's when I ran outside, unable to catch my breath, my entire body shaking uncontrollably. I was confused, angry. I'm not sure. After that, I wanted nothing to do with my father.

Is that why you stopped painting?

My father did very few interviews. But the ones he did, I must have read a hundred times. Isaias spoke about these vibrations that coursed through him. This powerful creative force that conjured waves of energy. An inner spark that buzzed through his body, into his fingertips, urging him to the canvas to paint. During his manic episodes, the energy would turn dark, as if shadows were creeping across that life force. He confessed that painting was the only thing that liberated him. That was how he released his demons to the void. Some of his best work came from that darkness. That's why he believed that his mental health and artistic gifts were so closely linked.

As I got older, I started to understand. I felt that energy inside me. The good and bad. I was diagnosed with mental health issues at an early age. For years, I felt like these storm clouds and shadows hovering over me. This horrible anxiety lingering in the background. Often, that darkness felt like a fortress between me and the rest of the world. But as long as I kept busy, as long as I didn't stop moving...

I too found therapy in my art. And like him, my best work came during my darkest moments. Like the night my mother passed. I was in our house alone, covered in these dark shadows. Like a foreign entity trapped inside my body. This weight on my chest just pressing down. That night, I painted. It came from a place utterly outside of myself, and yet completely within me. It was an abstract portrait of my mother, with bright brush strokes covering her eyes, my grief and sadness dripping out onto the canvas.

When I displayed the painting at a student art show, it was purchased by an anonymous buyer. One of only pieces that sold that night. My teachers and classmates were impressed. It should have been the start of my budding artistic career. But six months later, Wyatt's exhibit opened, and when I saw my dead father suspended in that liquid, I lost my will to paint. I lost that vibrational force, that connection to my father. In fact, I never wanted to feel it or let it consume me again. So I dropped out of art school, and I decided to dive into a new career in journalism. I used work to avoid everything.

JOSS: While Cal talked, Tony motioned to a spot on the ground, near Cal's feet. Underneath a small pile of rubble lay a business card.

CAL: I reached down and picked it up. The card was weathered and old, but it still held its form. It wasn't a traditional business card at all. Instead of a name, title, and address, it just read, "The Art Dealer." On the back, a symbol: XIIX.

CAL: On the day following the contestant selection, a new digital portrait appeared on the auction site DARK WATERS. The last four remaining influencers adorned in jumpsuits and ski masks holding their phones like weapons. The words: Meet your 'II' Ambassadors. Angel Asher. Kiki Kelly. Bella Allesandra and Sienna Owens.

BELLA ALLESANDRA: Not going to lie, I looked sexy as fuck in a ski mask. There was something powerful about being on Wyatt's team. I'd be the one inflicting pain and fear. On the third day, we were brought to the war room, a tented control center with a giant model replica of the island. There were a dozen monitors on the wall that displayed feeds from all the hidden cameras on the island. I'll never forget looking up at one monitor and seeing Wyatt's men sorting through a crate of knives and guns. I knew this shit was going to be a blood bath. I just didn't know how fucked up it was going to be.

Once our ambassador duties started, our regiment was more structured. We were required to wear ski masks at all times. We ate meals in silence with the other disciples. We were only allowed outside our tent during specific hours. A few days in, they handed us yellow folders with a photo of the contestant we would be mentoring, as well as instruction on the challenges we would be designing. Our job was to brand, market, and guide our contestants on their journey to fame and followers. We would solicit paid sponsorships to boost their popularity. You ever see *The Hunger Games*? We were basically the mentor and game makers rolled into one. **[LAUGHS]**

There was also a caveat. Our fate was tied to each contestant. If our contestant lost, so did we. And since there were only four ambassadors and ten contestants, well, not everyone would be getting sponsors and help, would they? Wyatt James knew exactly who he wanted at the end of this competition.

CARRIE: What can I say about the press tour? On the surface, it was a dream come true. Being styled in expensive outfits. Adorning the most prestigious magazine covers. But it didn't matter. I was lonelier, more isolated than ever.

I had a massive panic attack on the eve of our departure. I was in bed, just scrolling, and I realized that I didn't have any pictures of Tuck on my account anymore. There was nothing left of the girl I used to be before he went missing. It was all part of Kiana's agency's strategy to rebrand me. And before I knew it, my whole profile became these curated photos of a fake surfer girl in a bikini. But that wasn't me. This was not the girl that Tuck raised. I was an athlete. A competitor. Not some model posing in a thong bikini. Worse, if this was what my followers liked about me, I was a fraud.

That was when I decided to get in the car and drive.

CAL: Meanwhile.

BUZZFEED NEWS AUDIO CLIP: The mysterious competition known as Influencer Island has the internet buzzing once again.

BELLA ALLESANDRA: It was the middle of the night when I heard the lackeys talking and marching through the camp. I stepped out of my tent and saw Sienna and Angel poking their heads out as well. I whispered, "Where's Kiki?" Nobody knew. At that point, I knew she was done for.

LANE: So at 2:53 a.m. on Friday, literally the morning the competitors were supposed to leave for the island, influencer Kiki Kelly allegedly went live on her Gl!tch account. The thousands of users who saw the selfie-style video claim it had a very horror movie-like feel. With matted hair and bloodshot eyes, Kiki stumbled down the beach in her sports bra and shorts. In a shaky voice, she said, "They are going to kill us . . . They are going to kill us all." This was followed by a few cries and sniffles before she uttered a final warning: "Don't come to the island. It's a trap."

JOSS: Once Kiki Kelly posted that video, the public finally took the Redditors seriously. Everyone knew this thing was going to be a catastrophe.

LANE: Sadly, instead of outrage, the internet resorted to memes. Conjuring up all sorts of *Lord of the Flies* scenarios. Even more unsettling, Kiki Kelly's horror-esque warning became a trending sound bite on TikTok. As if this was one big joke.

BELLA ALLESANDRA:

Can you tell us what happened to Kiki?

She was the first ambassador to go into the box. An instrument of torture created by Wyatt James. His way of breaking us down. After they removed her, she wouldn't stop shaking, mumbling that she was sorry. We had no idea what she meant. Kiki was in no condition to compete. She was out of the competition before it even started.

What about you? Did you ever stand a chance?

Hindsight is twenty fucking twenty, right? As you must know by now, the conclusion was always inevitable. All deliberate. Beginning, middle, and end. No, I never stood a chance. This wasn't a competition. It was a pre-meditated massacre. All in the name of art.

CAL: As the contestants prepared to board a plane to the island, Joss and I were hard at work following clues related to the business card. Once again, we turned to Wyatt World, which had an entire thread dedicated to this so called "Art Dealer". He or she was the middleman between Wyatt's work and the art community. The Art Dealer sold more than two hundred real and digital pieces for Wyatt, including many of the ones excavated off buildings during the DIED FAMOUS installations. The Art Dealer's identity was a mystery.

The works were sold at covert underground events, exclusive gatherings for the rich and famous. Invite was by way of a business card, which we had. So far, there had been three documented events. One at an old prohibition-era bar beneath the city. One at an abandoned warehouse in Venice. And the last at a clandestine gallery in the Getty Museum. When and where the next auction was taking place was anyone's guess.

JOSS: As for the symbol on the back of the card—XII X—we couldn't find much. There were rumors floating around Wyatt World that it was some shadowy mark of the Hollywood elite. There were several conspiracies about it being linked to some dark entity. That it was related to the deaths of various celebrities, artists, and politicians—Van Gogh, Marilyn Monroe, Natalie Wood, just to name a few. The symbol added to Wyatt's mystique, that he was part of this dark, exclusive Illuminati society nicknamed "The Eleven."

CAL: We had been on Wyatt World for hours when Joss spotted a new thread. The Art Dealer had sent out word of an auction that would be taking place the next evening. Joss and I looked at each other in shock. We couldn't believe our luck. We had our ticket in —we just needed an address.

JOSS: It was midnight by the time we logged out of Wyatt World. I was on my way out when I heard a knock at Cal's door. I opened the door to find Carrie Andrews staring back at me, wearing nothing but pajama shorts and a tank top. I remember scoffing in her face before turning back to Cal, like—*I hope you know what you're doing.*

CARRIE: It was the night before we were going to the island. I was scared. What if I never came back? I didn't want to spend my last night alone.

CAL: When Carrie showed up at my house that night, I knew she was upset. We didn't talk much. We didn't have to. I just held her close and told her that everything was going to be okay. She rolled over to me in the middle of the night and asked. *Do you promise? Do you promise everything is going to be okay?* I said yes. Looking back, it was a shitty thing for me to say. Maybe I should have prepared her for the worst. Maybe I was fooling myself. She trusted me. I let her down like everyone else in her life.

I woke up at 7:00 a.m. to the sound of my alarm. Carrie was already gone. When I grabbed my phone, I noticed five missed calls and two text messages from Joss. She said: *Tuck's phone records came back. You're going to want to see this.*

JOSS: While Cal was busy cuddling, I got evidence that every contestant on that island was chosen for a very specific reason. They all had a connection to Tuck Andrews.

CARRIE: On the morning of our flight, thousands of fans camped out at the private hangar in Burbank to watch us depart for the island. None of us truly grasped how big this thing was. We were pop stars embarking on a world tour with screaming fans holding up posters with our names on them. Paparazzi taking pictures. Interviews on the red carpet. It was just like Wyatt promised. We were larger than life.

AUDIO FROM RUNWAY INTERVIEW
E! NEWS REPORTER: Nicki Mo, Nicki Mo! What do you think the competition is going to be?
NICKI MO: C'mon, darlin'. What do you think? We're going to hunt each other for sport. Shoot and skin each other like animals. Maybe look pretty while we do it. Get a few likes along the way. And from the looks of these other contestants, I like my chances.

CAL: I must have dialed and redialed Carrie a hundred times. But every time it rang once and went straight to voicemail. Joss had relayed the contents of Tuck's phone records, evidence that LAPD overlooked. I needed to warn Carrie. According to Joss's insider, everyone on that plane, besides Carrie and Kiana, messaged Tuck the word, "Cheshire" on the night of his disappearance. Joss's insider also found a report of an eyewitness who saw Tuck on the night he disappeared. He described Tuck's outfit, a cutoff shirt with black jeans. The same outfit he wore in the picture with Kiana, which meant she and Tuck must have been together that night. I arrived at the hangar ten minutes before takeoff, shoving my way through the crowd, screaming Carrie's name. By the time I made it to the tarmac, it was too late. Wheels were up.

CARRIE: Once we got on the private plane, they took our phones and replaced them with new ones. The only application on it was Gl!tch. I remember sitting next to Kiana, taking a selfie. It was a cute pic. But when I zoomed in, Kiana's face was rigid and stiff. Do I think she knew what awaited us? No. But she came to the island for a reason. We all had secrets and demons.

LANE: Once they left that hangar, no one could save these poor kids. They were in the hands of Wyatt James.

AGENT COOPER: We tracked the flight as soon as it left Los Angeles. They went offline somewhere over the Atlantic. We expected that. But there was nothing we could do. Only after the first confirmed homicide were we given the war chest.

CAL: As the contestants jetted off to the island, I went straight back to BlueLA HQ to meet Joss. We had work to do. There was something larger at play that we needed to expose. Why did everyone on that plane text Tuck Andrews on the night of his disappearance? How was Kiana Martin involved? And why would Wyatt James put together this specific group of people? These questions were eating me alive. Anxious to get to the bottom of Wyatt's plans, our first contact was an up-and-coming actor named Zan Silvers

JOSS: When I first started working at BlueLA, I interviewed Zan in his Malibu home. He had a gorgeous view, but even more impressive was his incredible art collection. One piece in particular caught my eye—a Wyatt James portrait of Natalie Wood, which was graffitied on the side of an old yacht in Marina Del Ray. The piece of rusty steel was removed from the ship and now sat behind glass on Zan's wall. He was proud to show it off. A Wyatt James piece wasn't easy to get your hands on.

After Cal and I discovered that the Art Dealer was holding a secret art auction that night, I called Zan to get more information. And boy, did he have a story to tell.

CAL: According to Zan, the invitation to Wyatt's auctions were extremely exclusive. You were handed a business card with the symbol XIIX from a stranger at a random time. Then, guests were notified in a cryptic message on their phone, which when clicked, flashed the location for two seconds before disappearing. When you arrived, you handed your business card over to someone named Virgil, who Zan referred to as "the guide," someone in plain sight. Zan said he received a message that day. An auction was taking place at the Hollywood Roosevelt Hotel at midnight, sharp.

JOSS: It made sense that the auction would be at the Roosevelt. It was the oldest hotel in Los Angeles and had its fair share of celebrity drama and death. A landmark fitting for Wyatt James.

CAL: Joss and I arrived with five minutes to spare, racing through the grand lobby of the hotel. Joss was the first to spot "the guide," a cleaning crew member in the empty lobby with a name-tag that said "Virgil." A part of me thought this was a practical joke being played on us.

JOSS: But it wasn't. The attendant took the card without the slightest hesitation. As if he was expecting us. He led us to a decorative library in an alcove, glancing around suspiciously before unlocking a hidden door built into the bookshelf.

CAL: The secret door was part of the hotel's intriguing history. Beneath the ground floor was a hidden basement theater where several strange burlesque and magic shows have been held over the years. As soon as it opened, we saw a man in a gold ski mask standing in a long, mirrored hallway. He held out a tray with two black ski masks. Then he motioned for us to place our cell phones on the tray before he invited us onward. I don't think my heart has ever raced faster in my life.

CARRIE: After a five-hour flight, the island came into view. It was the perfect little paradise. Gorgeous teal waters, white sandy beaches, all framed by a stunning sunset. Influencer Island was real. As soon as we landed on the overgrown tarmac, two Jeeps pulled up with masked drivers at the wheel. I'm not sure what I imagined. Maybe we'd be taken to party on the beach. Given a few cocktails while we settled in, you know? But the Jeep drove us along a bumpy jungle road to Wyatt's little military camp. I'll never forget the smell in the air. Like death. Sulfur and rotting flesh. You couldn't help but feel like we were entering the devil's lair. I reached for Kiana's hand as we drove past two masked guards with guns.

What happened next?

We were brought to a tent for a meet and greet with our ambassadors. These were models I'd been following for years. I used to watch Kiki Kelly work the runaway at the Victoria's Secret Fashion Show. But standing six feet away from them, I don't know. It was unnerving. I noticed Kiki's hand shaking as she tried to put a martini glass to her mouth. When the glass fell from her hand and shattered, she winced like she was about to be punished. Internally, every siren was going off.

Then Angel Asher came into the tent **[SMILING]** She put me at ease. I've always envied Angel. In some ways, I feel like she took the life I was supposed to have. We were raised on the same beaches. Our high schools were only five blocks apart. We were both the top surfers in our division. And in one moment, our lives took completely different paths. So many times, after getting off a grueling shift at the café, I'd just sit and stare at Angel's account, scrolling through photos of her posing on one exotic beach after the other. I was so envious. And there she was, standing right in front of me. The woman my brother taught me was the competition. But if I'm being honest, I was starstruck.

Angel scooped me away and led me outside, where we strolled under the tiki torch light. She told me not to tell anyone, but she was my ambassador. She would be guiding me through the competition. Then she leaned in, like she didn't want anyone to hear what she was going tell me. She warned me, "Someone is always watching." She told me to never forget that. If I was dancing, then dance like millions of people were tuned in, because they will be. Then she poured me a glass of champagne to make a toast. She said she was so sorry to hear about my brother, that she was always fond of him. He had even trained her for a few months after my accident.

Did you know Tuck trained Angel?

No idea. And I hated the way she said it, too. Like she was throwing it in my face. Like she knew that he withheld that secret from me. Turns out, Tuck kept a lot more than that from me. That was just the tip of the iceberg.

CAL: The air was stale and rancid as we walked down a hall of mirrors, which funneled us into a dingy, poorly lit theater. Seated in rows of timeworn velvet booths were at least fifty people with black ski masks, smoking cigars and drinking liquor. Auction paddles were brought to us on silver trays.

JOSS: Hidden identities or not, you could just feel the power and money lurking in that room.

CAL: At a minute past midnight, the curtain opened and a slender masked figure in a black dress and heels stood before us— the Art Dealer. She wasted no time. The first piece was brought forth by attendants. An intimate portrait of a heavyset man with two hollowed-out eyes, his pupils hidden behind a thin version of Wyatt's signature blur. In his left hand, he gripped a bible and a knife. In the other, his fingers locked in a snapping position. The Art Dealer explained that this piece was from Wyatt's newest series, "Power." The painting was entitled "Snap & Kill," in reference to the boss of a crime syndicate who ordered the death of over a thousand people by snapping his fingers. The bidding started at five hundred thousand dollars.

JOSS: Piece by piece, the attendees raised their paddles. Each portrait was shocking and disturbing. Wyatt James traveled far and wide to find the most powerful, dangerous people in the world—warlords, cartel members, billionaires, and corrupt businessmen. After seven of these paintings, the Art Dealer moved on to some of James's older pieces, including paintings of a few recognizable celebrities.

CAL: I kept looking around, hoping to find some clue, something that could help us identify the people in the room. I feared that we might leave with nothing. And then they brought the final painting onto the stage. My entire body went numb.

JOSS: It was a painting of Cal's father. One of the original eleven that Wyatt painted for the installation. This one was entitled "The Seeker," and it was a picture of Isaias staring off into the distance, with pieces of his skin flaking off his face. The bidding started at a million dollars.

CAL: My mind and heartbeat raced as I watched everyone raise their paddles. I couldn't stand the thought of someone buying a portrait of my father. His face on a vanity decoration in some billionaire's posh penthouse. Without hesitation, I raised my paddle. And I made my bid with no intention of ever handing over any money.

JOSS: I whispered to Cal, "What are you doing?" But even though I couldn't see his face behind the mask, I knew he wasn't going to stop. The bidding was up to three million dollars.

CAL: I was bidding against one other person, who finally conceded. Then the Art Dealer pointed at me and yelled, "Sold." That's when it hit me. What was I going to do when I claimed the painting?

CARRIE: At seven o'clock, each influencer was escorted to separate tents to prepare for the opening ceremony. Wyatt had placed a terrifying painting above the vanity in my tent. It was a pale-faced, frightened maiden stranded on a dark, algae-covered rock in the middle of the sea. And climbing out of the ocean onto the rock is this horned demon, a red and black scaly looking creature with hideous fangs. That painting still haunts me. **[DEEP IN THOUGHT]** I was the maiden and the demon.

An hour before the ceremony started, Angel came in with my sponsored outfit for the night, along with three other masked stylists. To her credit, it was an incredible choice. A tropical St. Terrance dress with gorgeous nude heels. As the stylists did my makeup in the mirror, Angel stood behind me, examining every detail of my outfit. As if one smudge of makeup could decide my fate. When they finished, armed men came in to escort me to the opening ceremony. But before I walked out, Angel grabbed my hand and looked me straight in the eyes. She said, "From here on out, you do everything I tell you. You trust me, no matter what."

LANE: So there I was, in my cubicle at work, totally glued to my phone, when I saw the Influencer Island account go live. When I clicked on the icon, a two-minute countdown began. The backdrop was a golden carpet with tiki torches at each side. As soon as the two minutes were up, the tiki torches flamed out and everything went pitch black.

CARRIE: One by one, cell phone lights illuminated a gold carpet. Each contestant stepped onto the path, in order of their invitation. I was last. I looked to my left, then right, trying to get a glimpse of the faces hidden in the shadows. And then the music began. That dramatic theme song. Those heavy drums booming over us, rattling the nerves inside my stomach.

LANE: All around the world, users were watching the opening ceremony from their phones. From various live feeds on Gl!tch. From the accounts of the biggest influencers in the world, who were recording the entire thing. If you combine the total number of viewers from each account, it was over fifty million—one of the highest watched opening shows of all time.

CARRIE: The carpet led us to the cliff's edge, where our host, Kaylyn Jenson lit two torches and stood to face us. She was wearing a tight glittery dress with red lipstick, her long black hair waving in the warm, island breeze. With a snap of her fingers, all the influencers left their positions and came towards us. That was when we saw who was holding the cell phones. **[PAUSES, SMILES]** The most recognizable faces in the world.

JOSS: Kaylyn Jenson introduced the contest live on Gl!tch.

AUDIO FROM KAYLYN JENSON: Welcome to Influencer Island, a transformative experience to see if you have what it takes to influence the masses. Tonight, it's important that you prove that you belong. At the end of the night, one of you will be eliminated.

[MURMURS IN CROWD]

I must warn you. This island is full of dark and dangerous secrets, including a mysterious eleventh competitor who will conceal themselves until the right time. But for now, I will present our contestants with a question: How far would you be willing to go for fame and followers?

CARRIE: As soon as she said it, there was this long pause, like she was letting the question sink in. As if we needed to answer right then and there.

AUDIO FROM KAYLYN JENSON: Contestants, this is your first test. Beyond this stage, the competition awaits. Who will take the first step into the unknown?

CARRIE: It was at least a hundred feet or higher from the cliff to the ocean. If that didn't kill us, surely the jagged rocks on the way down would. And yet. As the phones kept recording, there was a part of me that *needed* to prove myself. I was the adventurous beach girl. Diving off cliffs was part of my brand. I wanted my followers to be proud of me. My heartbeat pounded in my chest as I looked over at Angel. She nodded, and her words rattled in my head. *From here on out, do everything I tell you.* And that's when I said it.

AUDIO FROM 'II' ACCOUNT [CARRIE ANDREWS]: I'll do it.

CARRIE: I removed my heels and stepped onto the edge of the cliff, my entire body shaking. I chickened out. No amount of adrenaline would get me to jump. Kiana leaned into my ear, whispering, "You don't have to do this." And just when I was about to turn back, I felt a set of hands shove me forward. I was free falling into darkness.

BELLA: Angel was the one who shoved her off. She would do anything to win.

JOSS: When Cal bought the painting, the tension thickened in the room. A masked man came on stage and whispered something in the Art Dealer's ear. She gazed out across the theater, straight at Cal. Our cover was blown.

CAL: You read Wyatt World long enough, you're bound to be paranoid. Whoever these people were, they went to great lengths to keep their secrets. Eventually, everyone stood up and began filing out of the room. Joss and I followed suit. When we got to the door, a masked man stopped us.

JOSS: As an ambitious journalist, I've put myself in some dangerous situations. Some seedy neighborhoods with unsavory folks. But there was just something so creepy about rich people wearing fucking ski masks.

CAL: We were asked to follow the Art Dealer backstage, into a velvet-lined hallway, with all sorts of old Hollywood photos along the wall. I was so thankful when I saw a busted EXIT sign hanging above a door. I thought, maybe, just maybe, they were just going to send us off with a warning.

JOSS: When she opened the door to the street, there was a limo in an alleyway, the engine running. A masked man was leaning against the car. He ordered Cal to get in the backseat. When Cal refused, he pulled back his jacket to reveal a gun in his waistband.

CAL: Despite being held at gunpoint, there was something exhilarating about it all. This was the closest I had ever been to the secret world of Wyatt James. I was one step closer to confronting my father's killer.

JOSS: I tried to follow Cal, but when I made my move, the driver stopped me. He pointed at Cal as if to say, "He's the one we want." Then the door slammed, and they drove away. I wasn't sure I would ever see Cal again.

CARRIE: Darkness. That was all I remember. It was all consuming. The landing felt like I was smashing into cold, dark, asphalt. This surge of pain swam up and down my body. Once submerged, memories of my surf accident flashed across my mind. My leg being crushed, tumbled over and over. The long hand of the waves ripping me under, never letting go. By the time I made it to the surface, I was gasping for air, bobbing up and down in the dark waters.

Then I saw another body crash into the water. Kiana's face popped up shortly after, screaming in excitement. All I felt was relief. We were alive. She pointed away from the cliff and told me to swim. As soon as we made it around the bend, I saw the lights and music from a nearby beach cover… It was the party we were promised.

LANE: The footage on the 'II' account made it look like one epic music video. Strobe lights flashing. Quick cuts of celebrities drinking and dancing. There were fifteen bars. DJ Mad DoX was spinning with his Mad Hatter top hat. Every top influencer was dancing and partying beneath the island stars and tiki torches. I started to imagine viewers around the world watching on a bus, in an Uber, at the dinner table. The greatest party ever curated.

BELLA ALLESANDRA: As soon we got into the party, the ambassadors got to work. It was up to us to start making alliances. A single endorsement could land our contestants another fifty thousand new followers. Then there were the brand sponsorships which gave us additional access to funds to boost our contestants' accounts. But there was just one little problem.

Carrie had become a fan favorite. The daring, adventurous surfer girl. Angel was spinning the shit out of her. They had everyone eating out of the palm of her hand. In no time, Carrie was pulling away from the rest of the field.

CARRIE: I remember the DJ putting on his headphones, waving his hands in the air and yelling, "Welcome to Influencer Island!" And then the beat dropped, and a second wave of influencers rushed in from the outskirts of the plaza. I got lost in the moment. If I close my eyes, I can still see all their faces, flashing in and out of the strobe lights. The beat pounding and pounding as the alcohol soaked into my body. Influencers with millions and millions of followers were reaching for their phones to take pictures with me. With *me*. Telling me that I was their favorite. Every time I looked at my phone, my follower count increased by thousands. This insane flood of new notifications and adoration. I was on the top of the world and the leaderboard...and then in an instant, it all changed.

CAL: As soon as I got in the car, the driver turned and handed me a blindfold. I said, "Where are we going?" But the man said nothing. We drove in silence, onto the freeway, up steep, winding hills. About thirty minutes later, the car came to a halt. Then the door opened, and I was asked to remove my blindfold.

I was standing in some sort of compound or underground bunker, surrounded by bare concrete walls. Every conspiracy I ingested on Wyatt World was running on a loop in my head. A dangerous secret society responsible for countless murders with compounds all over the city. And now here I was, blindfolded and literally taken underground. So yeah, I was terrified.

I was led through a concrete hallway, until finally the driver scanned his security fob and opened the door to a cavernous gallery. It was possibly the greatest private art collection in the world. I recognized a few pieces right away—a Van Gogh, a Velazquez, a Rembrandt.

Then the sound of heels on cement echoed from the far end of the room. The Art Dealer walked toward me with her mask removed. She was elegant in her form-fitting black dress and heels, shimmering brown hair and perfect skin. I pegged her for early-to-mid-forties. She motioned for me to walk alongside her.

As we walked, two masked men moved past us holding the painting of my father, "The Seeker." After they hung it on the wall, the Art Dealer stopped, pausing to observe the piece. Because I didn't have a recording device, I've done my best to transcribe the conversation from memory.

THE ART DEALER [ACTRESS VO]: You are now in the private gallery of Wyatt James and a number of other powerful benefactors who I work for. As you know, Wyatt painted eleven pieces of your father, Isaias Everett, and to this day, he has never sold a single one. So imagine my surprise when this piece showed up at my office this morning. Of course, it came with a warning. That there would be an uninvited guest who would attempt to purchase the painting. And when they do, I was to bring them back to this gallery.

CAL: Not only did Wyatt know I would crash the auction, but he knew I would bid on the piece.

THE ART DEALER [ACTRESS VO]: I'm sorry to say that I do not have the answers you seek. I am simply a conduit, a middleman between their world and ours.

CAL: "Their world?" I asked. In response, she flashed her business card, with the familiar symbol—XIIX.

THE ART DEALER: Some say it represents the rich and powerful, the Gods of Hollywood. That the symbol leads the seeker to riches and triumphs beyond their wildest dreams. Others believe that the symbol is much bigger than that. That it represents death and destruction. That a terrible fate awaits anyone who seeks its true origins.

CAL: I asked, "How do I find them?"

THE ART DEALER: You don't; they find you. But there is a cost for the answers you seek. There is always a cost.

CAL: Then she motioned for me to continue walking through an archway to a small viewing room. Before I entered, the Art Dealer pulled out a small vial of clear liquid.

THE ART DEALER: Before you enter, you must drink this.

CAL: Why did I drink it? I was on the cusp of having my deepest questions answered. There was no turning back. As soon as I finished the drink, she invited me into the room and told me, "The answers you seek begin here."

CARRIE: One minute I was drinking tequila shots at the bar, and then, out of nowhere, everything gets hazy. This was the biggest night of my life, with millions of people watching, and I was drugged. Someone was out to get me.

BELLA ALLESANDRA: It was better than I could have imagined—watching Carrie take celebrity selfies with her tongue out, eyes half-mast. The curated Carrie was gone. Our favorite toilet girl had returned. Mascara dripping down her face. Swearing and cussing. She groped Trevor like he was a blowup doll at a bachelorette party. Within an hour, most of her sponsors and endorsements abandoned ship. I caught Angel trying to keep Carrie off camera a couple times. But this was Influencer Island. There was nowhere to hide. By 2:00 a.m., Wyatt's masked lackeys rounded up the ambassadors. It was time to put the contestants in position. As we headed toward the dance floor, two of them stopped Kiki and her contestant, Graham, throwing black bags over their heads. They were dragged into the jungle kicking and screaming.

CARRIE: It's all so blurry, but I remember looking across the party, and seeing him – Wyatt's masked face standing still amongst the crowd. I vaguely remember staggering in his direction, until I ended up in the darkness of the jungle. He was gone. But there was a photograph on the ground. A crinkled picture of my brother and me. It was the day he gave me my first surfboard, this used six-foot hard top with dried wax and faded stickers. Not a beginner's board at all. It was the first day he took me surfing. I was only seven years old, and he was a lanky thirteen-year-old with baggy board shorts and gelled spiked-up bleach hair. We were just kids. But when I examined the photo more closely, there was something wrong with our eyes, like someone had scratched them out... Again, it's just all so hazy.

LANE: Before the photographer, Graham, was eliminated, he posted this artsy photo of Carrie in the jungle, staring out into the darkness. And you can vaguely see an outline of a figure, a shadow. Was it Wyatt James? Who knows. But either way, the photo was telling. Carrie was chasing ghosts.

CARRIE: The last thing I remember? Kiana came and found me. She dragged me back to the dance floor. The rest of the influencers huddled around us, as if this was the culmination of the night. Like they were sending off a bride and groom at the end of a wedding reception. Their smiling faces kept coming in and out of focus. I vaguely recall Trevor's grotesque hands all over me on the dance floor, and then suddenly, everyone was screaming in celebration, their phones out, recording everything.

CAL: On the wall in front of me was *my* painting. The one I painted in art school. The one of my mother. And looking at it, after all these years, with whatever liquid poison was running through me, I saw my grief. These painful vibrations swirling off the canvas. These awful hallucinations. My mother's hollowed face floating towards me. Still, even amidst the terror, one question lingered in my mind: *Why was my painting in Wyatt's private gallery?*

CARRIE: Suddenly, I was spinning around in a panic, seeing faces fade in and out of focus. A remixed version of the contest theme song was on repeat in the background. I felt like I was underwater; the beat kept pounding and thumping in my head. Like I was drowning, desperately trying to swim to the surface. Everyone's screams stretched out to a drawl, the song's tempo slowed, and my eyes lost focus. As I staggered away from the dance floor, I saw Nicki Mo, Trevor, and Kiana get black bags thrown over their heads.

CAL: Whatever poison was in that cup began to really kick in. My vision blurred at the corners, and my legs and arms went numb. Someone walked into the room. He was tall and intimidating, with dark eyes and a low-brimmed hat. His voice was deep and menacing. I remember him staring at my painting, marveling at it. He asked me why I'd wasted such talent. I stumbled backward, unable to speak. Then he asked if I wanted the truth. If I wanted to know who Wyatt James was. And I nodded.

CARRIE: My body collapsed into the sand. Above me, the beautiful starry night sky swirled round and round as the music thumped in the background.

CAL: The next thing I remember is waking up on an airplane.

BELLA ALLESANDRA: The party was over. But as far as we were concerned, the work was just beginning.

CAL: I was headed to the island as a special guest of Wyatt James.

[PART 3]

THE CONTEST BEGINS

EPISODE SEVEN:

THE SWIM

CAL: On October 11th, nearly a week after the competition was over, Agent Michelle Cooper climbed the winding metal steps to an infamous lighthouse, the location of Influencer Island's final transmission. The place was cleaned out by forensics, but she could still see the dried blood stains on the cement floor, evidence of the contest's final showdown. Agent Cooper strolled to the edge of the platform, staring out across the island, at the vast ocean surrounding her. There was something she was hesitant to admit in her report back to Washington.

AGENT COOPER: You must understand. I was under ridiculous pressure. Everyone was breathing down our necks. The Pentagon, Homeland Security, every department was taking heat for this. Not to mention the public outcry. I had five hours to turn in my report.

What were you looking for in that lighthouse?

I had gotten the full story of what happened in those final moments of Influencer Island. Everything that wasn't caught on camera. Wyatt James's entire confession. But I couldn't put it in the report. I just couldn't believe it. Maybe I didn't want to believe it. I wasn't ready to untangle the thread that far. But just when I was about to leave, I spotted something shiny lodged in a small crack in the cement, a golden ring. I twirled it around in my hands, staring at the symbol etched into the metal—XIIX.

That's when I knew that Cal Everett was telling the truth. The organization called The Eleven were responsible for everything that transpired. I just needed to know how this installation furthered their cause.

JOSS: On the second day of the competition, the Influencer Island account posted photos of Kiki Kelly and contestant Graham Carter, two silhouettes with gold blurs covering their eyes. Their digital portraits were then auctioned off on the internet to the highest bidder. They were considered the first team to be eliminated.

BELLA ALLESANDRA: That elimination post was beyond dramatic, a still image of Kiki and her contestant's side profiles with the theme music playing in the background. It truly felt like we were living in a young adult dystopian novel.

And what about the other influencers who were flown in for the opening ceremony?

Those influencers were marched at gunpoint to their encampment. A fenced in sandbar with emergency tents and mattresses. **[CHUCKLES, SMILES]** I'm not going to say I didn't enjoy watching them all sniffle and cry as they were thrown into the camp. It's not like they didn't have food and water.

You sound like you enjoyed working for Wyatt James?

It was a different kind of power. More absolute. Better than fame or influencing my followers to buy shit. That's just preying on insecurities. This fear ran deep. The public isn't going to hear these interviews, right?

LANE: As soon as photos and videos began leaking from the imprisoned influencers, the internet lost their mind. The public fell into two camps. You were either up in arms about your favorite creators and influencers being held captive, or you thought they were getting what they deserved. **[LAUGHS]** But the ratings spoke for themselves. This was a modern-day version of the Roman Colosseum. The internet wanted blood. Everyone tuned in.

CARRIE: When I came to, I noticed the chalky taste of sand in my mouth. My head was pounding like a cheap speaker. All the other contestants were scattered around me on the beach, gingerly sitting up. The females were dressed in skimpy golden bikinis and the guys in knee-length frayed shorts. I turned to find my phone in the sand, buzzing with notifications. It was exactly what I feared. Tagged in one meme after the next. My drunken antics on display for the entire world. There were videos of me screaming at the top of my lungs, burying my face into all these celebrities. Swearing. Yelling. Worst of all, kissing Trevor. All my endorsements and sponsors had left me for other contestants. I was in last place. As soon as I looked up from my phone, Kiana plopped next to me in the sand.

AUDIO FROM 'II' ACCOUNT:

KIANA: Is gold my color? **[SPINNING AROUND]**
CARRIE: What the fuck happened last night?
KIANA: Looks like you couldn't resist Trevor's charm.
CARRIE: That's not funny. Where were you?
KIANA: I'm sorry. I didn't know I was back on chaperone duty.
CARRIE: I wasn't' that drunk. I think I was drugged.
KIANA: You're being paranoid.
CARRIE: There's something strange going on. I

saw something last night. There was this photo of Tuck and I.
[LONG PAUSE]
KIANA: You need to stop with this shit, Carrie. Not everything is about Tuck. You ever think you're imagining it?
CARRIE: What is your problem? Ever since this competition started. You've been impossible to get a hold of. It's like you don't give a shit about me anymore.

CARRIE: Kiana was just about to say something when our phones started buzzing. All the contestants were tagged in a video.

AUDIO FROM KAYLYN JENSON: Welcome to day one of the competition. Influencing is all about adding value to your followers. It's up to you to create an electric, addictive, personal brand that can persuade the masses.

Make sure you get your follower count and engagement up. The bigger your following, the more of an advantage you'll have in the challenges to come. And trust me, you're going to need it. Good luck, contestants. As always, may fame and followers be upon you.

CARRIE: Before I could say anything to Kiana, she got up and stormed away. The next few hours dripped like wax. There are only so many live sessions and scrolling you can do when your battery is less than 20%. There wasn't much to report anyway. Unless you wanted to see Trevor doing a makeshift island workout, or Nicki Mo sharpening a wooden stick to go fishing. I did the best I could to gain traction, going live to my followers and apologizing for my antics. I even promoted the one sponsor that had stuck around, Coco Smoothie, who delivered me a meager chocolate smoothie for breakfast. By noon, I found myself down at the shore, watching the waves. That was when I noticed four surf-boards with camera phones mounted on the front. In the distance, four rocks surrounded by a barbed-wire fence. Andrea came and joined me at the shoreline.

AUDIO FROM 'II' ACCOUNT:
ANDREA: It's going to be a bloodbath.
CARRIE: What?
ANDREA: I tapped into the island camera system. There are over five thousand cameras on this island and some of them are underwa-ter. Look.

CARRIE: When she turned her phone around, I witnessed a cluster of great white sharks frantically swimming underwater. On cue, our phones rang with another notification.

AUDIO FROM KAYLYN JENSON: Hello, contestants, and welcome to our first challenge. It's time to separate the influencers from the posers. Sexy surfers know how to get social engage-ment. Waves, actions, and picturesque beaches are a recipe for Gl!tch success.

In this challenge, you'll swim out to a fenced-in rock. There, you will find a back-pack full of rations, as well as a new phone that you need to keep you in the competition. Of course, there's just one little problem. There are only four rocks, and inside the fence will be eleven great white sharks.

To complete the challenge, you'll have to swim
through the shark-infested area and get to a
rock before the other competitors. And unfor-
tunately for you, these sharks have been
intentionally starved. Which means they will
be hungry for influencer chum. Based on the
current follower count, Thalia Grey will be
first to enter the water and Carrie Andrews
will be last. Good luck.

LANE: I remember exactly where I was when the announcement was made. I was cooking a risotto in my kitchen, a spatula in one hand, a glass of cabernet in the other. As soon as Kaylyn Jenson said it, the wine glass fell and shattered on the floor.

BELLA ALLESANDRA: Angel was the one who designed the first competition. **[SNICKERS]** The blood is on her hands.

JOSS: During those first hours, I was locked in my office, still trying to piece everything together. Desperately trying to figure out what Wyatt had planned for Cal. The rest of the company was watching the contest on a projector in the main workspace. There was a keg of beer, pizza, snacks, the works. I was staring at the investigation board in my office when Tony screamed. "Joss, you're going to want to come and see this! The contestants are about to be eaten alive!"

CARRIE: Everyone quickly came to the shore and crowded around Andrea's phone.

AUDIO FROM 'II' ACCOUNT:
DAN: Is this a fucking joke?
ANDREA: I found a dock a mile down the beach
with four jet skis. I say we make a run
for it.
TREVOR: You just want everyone to leave so you
can win.

ANDREA: This isn't a game anymore.

TREVOR: What about you, blondie? You're a surfer. You like your chances?

[TREVOR GOES TO GRAB CARRIE'S ASS. SHE SHOVES HIM AWAY.]

TREVOR: Ohhh, feisty. You weren't so reserved last night.

CARRIE: Because you fucking drugged me.

TREVOR: Please. I didn't need to drug you. You were all over *me*.

ANDREA: Everyone shut the FUCK UP! I've seen the footage around the island. There's a lot more in store for us. This is only the beginning.

NICKI MO: It's about time we got to the fun part.

DANIELLE: You're a psycho bitch.

THALIA: I'm not going in that water. I can barely swim.

CARRIE: As we were all discussing, a robotic voice echoed across the beach from speakers attached to palm trees.

AUDIO FROM 'II' ACCOUNT: Contestants, the competition begins in ten seconds.

CARRIE: We were all looking around, still unsure what was happening.

AUDIO FROM 'II' ACCOUNT: Contestant number four, Thalia, prepare yourself.

CARRIE: Then the countdown started from ten. All of us stared at Thalia, the shorter of the London models. She sat there in silence, shaking from head to toe, her eyes like a deer in headlights. *Five, four, three, two, one.* A loud horn reverberated through the air. Thalia's feet were glued to the sand, her teeth chattering uncontrollably. I felt bad for her. But what were we going to do? Then, out of nowhere, she made a beeline down the shore. Sprinting toward the dock in her bathing suit. None of us tried to stop her. We figured she'd be disqualified. And then we heard a gunshot reverberate through the air. **[PAUSES]** It all happened so fast. One minute she was running down the beach, the next she was lying motionless in the sand. Her sister, Tia, shrieked, and all of us stood there in absolute shock.

LANE: Based on the comments, I still don't think anyone understood what happened. It almost felt like they were watching a fake reality show, or a murderous HBO episode, because everyone was just posting laughing emojis. Or maybe they did know what happened to that poor girl. Which says a lot about our culture, right?

CARRIE: Before we could process Thalia's murder, the speaker rang up gain.

AUDIO FROM 'II' ACCOUNT: Contestant number five, Tia. Prepare yourself.

CARRIE: This time, when the gunfire rang out, Tia slowly waded in the water with tears streaming down her face. I knew she wasn't going to survive. She could barely lift the surfboard up off the sand. One by one, the speaker announced every contestant's name. The first four leaders swept up the surfboards. I was thankful Kiana got a board. She winked at me before she went into the water. She was a strong swimmer. I knew she'd be safe. But everyone else—most of them weren't going to make it, even with a board. My heart was beating out of my chest as I watched each contestant paddle out. I hadn't been on a surfboard in years. How was I going to cover all that ground? I was going to fucking die. That's all I could think about as I frantically read the comments on my phone. *Did you see Tia? The shark's already feasting. You're next, Carrie. Bye bye surfer girl. I love your ass.* I was having a panic attack, the phone trembling in my hand, my lungs desperate for air, when suddenly, I saw a comment from a familiar user. Cheshire89.

"This is your ticket out."

[SMILING]

It was something Tuck used to say to me. He said it to me on the day he gave me my first surfboard. He bent down so he was eye level and he said, "This is your ticket out. Out of Newport. Out of our toxic fucking family. Out of everything."

So when Cheshire89 sent me that message, I knew Kiana was wrong. I wasn't imagining things. My brother was on this island. The realization sent a rush of adrenaline flooding into my body. The same feeling I used to get before every competition. Laser focused. The sound of the horn was music to my ears as I sprinted into the bloody waves.

CAL: Meanwhile, my plane touched down on the remote island. Two things were running through my head as I stepped out. Helping Carrie survive and finding Wyatt James. I was greeted on the runway by Kaylyn Jenson, who was standing there with two envelopes in her hand. She was instructed to offer me a choice. As if Wyatt James read my mind. One envelope contained information on Carrie's whereabouts, and the other was information that would lead me to Wyatt James. . . Information about my father.

According to Kaylyn, Isaias Everett's last days were spent on this island. And clues to his death and Wyatt's involvement were in that envelope. If I'm being honest, no matter how bad I wanted to confront Wyatt James, my thoughts were on Carrie. I wanted to do everything in my power to help her, warn her. But before I could grab the envelope, Kaylyn flipped her camera around and showed me videos of Carrie and the muscly contestant kissing at the party.

That's when you chose the other envelope?

I let my emotions get the better of me. I think about that moment all the time. What if I had found her on that beach that morning? What if I told her the truth about this competition? Maybe I could have saved her. **[PAUSE]** We all know what route both of us chose.

The envelope Kaylyn gave me was a map, which took me through the center of the island. I hiked through the thick, jungle trail for hours, my thoughts spinning. Had I made the right decision? What was going to happen to Carrie and the rest of the contestants? By dusk, I trudged into a small clearing where I found an abandoned shack swallowed up by the jungle. I had to pull back thick vines just to get to the decrepit door.

As I crept inside, I called out, "Is anyone here?" There was no response. The place was totally rotted out. The only thing inside was a blank canvas and barstool. I wondered if this was some sort of creepy makeshift studio that Wyatt James painted in. Then I heard footsteps outside. Someone was coming. I stood quietly, waiting for the door to open.

Then the footsteps stopped. I thought, *this is it. He has come for me.* But no one came. The sound of a hammer slamming down on a nail echoed through the shack. The door was being sealed shut. Another whack of the hammer. The truth left a sinking feeling in my gut. I was being trapped inside.

CARRIE: I entered the water with a lot of ground to cover. It had been years since I swam, but the muscle memory kicked in as my hands cut rhythmic motions through the waves. I dipped through the first break, feeling the powerful waves crash over my body. As soon as I emerged, I saw a board bobbing up and down in the water. No contestant nearby. I quickly hopped onboard the surfboard.

From the mounted camera, I followed the comments while I paddled. People were making predictions who was going to be eaten next. And most of them were hoping it was me. That's one thing you should know—I respond when people want me to fail. It's when people stop caring that I get complacent. That's why I thrived as a young surfer. Because all those other girls wanted me to eat shit. It was just my brother and me against the world. After the accident, I retreated. I lost my motivation. But seeing those comments, seeing people expecting me to fail, that inner drive reignited. I felt like my old self for the first time in years.

LANE: Kiana, Nicki Mo, and Andrea were the first ones to roll through the gate, followed by the Vegas couple, Dan and Danielle, who were paddling on the same board. They must have paddled about five feet inside the gate when a great white shark emerged from the depths, its jaw fully extended. When it crashed down, both of them were knocked off the board. Everyone online heard the screams. They saw Dan's arm torn from his body. They saw the pool of blood. The sharks tearing at him underwater. You couldn't fake that scene.

CARRIE: By the time I made it into the fenced enclosure, I was swimming through fiberglass debris and blood. From the cameras, I saw Kiana and Nicki Mo climb safely to the rocks. Andrea was nearing the third rock, which meant my only shot was the final rock. And my competition was Trevor. Despite his head start, he was no match for me. His thick muscles were weighing him down. But just when I was about to pass him, I felt something moving beneath us. We locked eyes just as the jaws emerged from the water. It felt like slow motion, its teeth clamping down on Trevor's board, snapping it in half. No matter how tough he pretended to be, his screams were just like everyone else's. Piercing and full of terror.

When he resurfaced, he was holding a sliver of his broken board. I could tell from his pale face, and the blood pooling in the water that he was injured. He wasn't going to make it. Another set of shark fins were closing in on us. That's when I made the decision to save him.

CAL: I anxiously paced the decrepit shack, kicking and punching the rotting wood. But it was useless. There was no way out. As soon as I gave up hope of escape, I noticed something shiny in the corner. Something I recognized. Something that belonged to my father—a heavy gold ring with a small skull. From old polaroids, I knew that my father used to wear it on his left thumb. As I spun the ring in my hand, I saw the symbol XIIX carved into the metal. The same symbol from the Art Dealer's business card. Was my father part of the same cult as Wyatt James? As I held it with my shaky hands, the ring fell from my grasp, into a small hole in the floorboard. When I scrambled to retrieve it, I noticed that a board was loose. I pulled it open to find a secret compartment under the floor. There at the bottom was an old leather-bound journal.

The pages were water-logged and full of mold, but the binding was intact. When I opened the first page, my father's initials stared back. I started reading my father's entries.

ENTRY 1: This is a log of my final descent into darkness. I have chosen this island for a reason. It has a rich history of evil and tragedy. Other artists have used the shadows that lurk here for their own transformation, including the writer Frederick Charles, who came here in exile. His bones were discovered a mile away from this very cottage. Next to his corpse was his final and greatest piece of work, a novel that would define his legacy. I have come here do the same. To paint my final masterpiece. To make peace with my demons. I have come to this island to die.

ENTRY 2: I have been staring at a canvas for twenty-four hours. I have always feared the blank canvas. The raw potential and pure possibility. What if the divine no longer whispers to me? I must practice patience. In two days' time, my apprentice will arrive on the island with my son. He shall help me perform an ancient ceremony. He shall help me create my final masterpiece.

CAL: I took a second to process what I read. My father wanted me to be with him in his final days. And then came the big question. Why had I never received an invitation?

CARRIE: Against my better judgment, and the internet's opinion, I paddled over to Trevor and screamed at him to get on the board. His body added another two hundred pounds, but I kept my eye on the rock, padding with the same strength and determination that once made me a champion. I kept waiting for the next attack, waiting for our bloody end, but it never came. When I made it to the rock, I dragged Trevor onto the jagged surface and away from danger. Then I assessed his wound. His leg was bitten badly, and the blood was still pouring out. He wouldn't survive long. "Hold on," I screamed, as I rushed up the rock, frantic to get to the backpack of supplies. There must be something in there that could stop the bleeding. **[SHAKING HEAD]** But I never made it to the bag. I felt something go straight through my leg, through the layers of tissue in my calf. When I looked down, a fiberglass shard of surfboard was sticking out of my leg. Trevor climbed to a standing position. Only one of us was making it off this rock alive.

CAL: This was my father's next journal entry:

ENTRY 3: The fast prepared my body for the venom. Tonight, I begin the ancient ceremony. I will be bitten by the fangs of the native snake. The poison will sweep through my body and bring my soul into eternal darkness. I will be embarking on this journey alone. My apprentice arrived this morning with disappointing news. My son has denied my invitation. I must paint my masterpiece without him.

And that was it. I searched frantically for more pages, but the log was finished. Everything else was ripped out. It was dusk by then, and I was deep in thought, pondering this mysterious invitation that I never received, when I heard a hissing sound. Then another, echoing upon itself. Hundreds of black snakes poured into the shack from a hidden compartment in the wall. I pressed my back against the far corner, desperately trying to retreat. There was nowhere to run. Nowhere to hide.

The entire floor was covered in wriggling, black venomous snakes, piles of slithering knots. My eyes darted for higher ground, to the only furniture in the shack, a rickety barstool in front of the blank canvas. I made a quick decision, leaping over the incoming tide of snakes and heading for it.

It could have been ten minutes or three hours for all I knew. I just sat there, completely still, staring at the blank canvas in front of me. I was terrified; the snakes slithering up and down my legs, hissing in agitation. And then I felt it. A lone snake found its way up the back of the barstool, gliding onto my thigh, up my back, and onto my neck.

The fangs penetrated deep into my skin, the thick venom dispersing through my veins. Within minutes, my body felt cold and heavy. Then a rush of fear and terror swelled inside me, and horrible images rose. Everything I'd pushed down for years. Images of my mother's pale, shrunken body in her final days. My father floating in that clear blue liquid. Unrecognizable images from my subconscious. Hooded figures chanting over me, speaking in Latin. Future images of me dying alone in my house. All my darkest thoughts, all the loneliness, the abandonment, the feeling of being unwanted, all those fears collided into a dark mass, and its shadowy energy smothered me like a pillow over my face.

CARRIE: With the shard sticking out of my leg, I slipped and fell onto the wet, jagged rock. Trevor saw his opening. He leaped on top of me, his veins bulging from his neck. He grabbed a rock and slammed it into my head. The cold blood dripped down my face, but the adrenaline stopped the pain from coming. He must have thought I was unconscious because he moved past me, limping to the bag of supplies. It took me a second to get my bearings and drag my body to a standing position. By then, Trevor was nearly at the bag. He would have gotten to it if it weren't for the gunshot that rang out in the distance. It startled him enough to turn around, and when he did, a smile twisted across his face.

AUDIO FROM 'II' ACCOUNT:
TREVOR: It's over, Blondie. The backpack is mine. If they don't kill you after, I will.
CARRIE: You can grab the backpack, but I already have the phone. That's what you need to stay in the competition. **[HOLDS UP HAND]**
TREVOR: Give me that fucking phone, bitch!

CARRIE: It wasn't a phone. It was a black rock about the same size. But my brother taught me a thing or two about balance. The tiniest shift in weight can cost you the perfect wave. I threw the rock just far enough to see Trevor lean his oversized upper body over to the right. The slight twist caused his weak leg to buckle, and he lost his balance. By the time he realized it was a rock, it was too late. His eyes went wide as he toppled over, crashing into the water. I didn't have to look. I heard what happened next. The sharks chewed his flesh until the screams disappeared.

CAL: I was fading into darkness, the venom sinking deeper and deeper. I thought I was going to die, but then, out of nowhere, I saw this flash, a distant ball of light. Followed by a temporary moment of clarity. Like I could see the fear and pain from a distance. I saw it for what it was—a foreign entity trapped inside me. And when it happened, I entered a mysterious vortex, where colors and raw energy swirled off everything. Instinctively, I reached for the paintbrush, and it felt like magic, just like my father described. Because with my hand on the brush, that bundle of fear and pain felt as if it were shooting out of my body and flowing into the instrument.

CARRIE: I didn't have time to think about Trevor. I was shivering uncontrollably, bleeding out of my left calf. Thankfully, the backpack was full of supplies. Bandages, rubbing alcohol, pain medication, energy bars, water, a knife, and a brand-new phone with a hundred percent battery. I checked the phone. An unread message from Angel appeared. It said, "Go live."

CAL: I truly felt like everything was purged from me onto the canvas. And in those paint strokes, I found freedom, all my fears being released from my soul. The darkness swirling from my subconscious straight into my hands. I knew I was hallucinating. But the energy, the buzzing in my fingertips. It all felt so real. I had no idea what I was painting.

CARRIE: Why did I get so emotional on the rock? I'd just endured a near-death experience. I was vulnerable. But you know what really stuck with me? It was that painting in my tent. The demon crawling up the rock. As if Wyatt had known I'd be in that position. As if he knew me better than I knew myself. And in that moment, I realized that the demon represented this fake bullshit person I created. This shell of a human, this imposter that had seized control of me. And I don't know, I just had this powerful urge to tell my truth.

AUDIO FROM CARRIE'S ACCOUNT: It's getting dark. Not sure how I'm going to get off this rock. Maybe this is as good a time as any to come clean. That was my first time on a surfboard in years. I know, I'm a fraud. . . All those magazine interviews. All the bullshit and lies. I haven't surfed a fucking day since my brother became a junkie. If you didn't know, my brother, Tuck Andrews, has been missing for over a year. I miss him every single day. He would be so disappointed in the girl you've followed these past weeks. He raised me to be better. And for some reason, I think he's still alive. I know this sounds crazy, but I think he's on this island.

LANE: That was a defining moment for Carrie. The facade of her perfect life melted away. Those types of vulnerable moments can define a brand. From there on out, people rooted for her. She had loyal fans. Fans that wanted her to find her brother. Fans who believed that maybe he *was* on the island.

AGENT COOPER: That was when I was first alerted of the Tuck Andrews case. There was a hashtag that started amongst Carrie's fans, #FindTuck. As soon as I looked into the details, I immediately knew something was off. Obviously, we didn't know how bizarre this case really was or how it was connected until the very end.

CARRIE: Telling my story on the rock was the first time that I didn't stare at the comments. Nor did I give a shit what people thought of me. I felt liberated. When it was over, I gazed out into the darkness, the phone turned off, just listening to the sound of the waves lapping against the rock. I was content—even though I had no idea how I would get to shore. Even though my calf was swollen and throbbing, and those sharks were still circling around, waiting to finish me off. Four rocks down, I heard Kiana's voice, singing, a tribute to the dead contestants. That's when reality set in. Only one of us was leaving this island alive.

CAL: I remember collapsing on the floor, the paintbrush falling from my hand. The poison drained me. The last thing I remember was looking up and staring back at Carrie's face on the canvas.

EPISODE EIGHT:

THE HUNT

WHY DO you think you painted Carrie in that shack?

CAL: **[SHRUGS]** I imagined that in my altered state, I would have painted a portrait of my mother, maybe my father. Instead, I just saw her...Carrie. In the same vein of Wyatt James and my father, I didn't paint her eyes. I created these wild brush strokes of red and orange. Painting Carrie was my way of saying that I wanted to choose a different path. I was tired of chasing ghosts.

When I came to, I was lying on the floor of the shack with the door wide open. I wasn't sure how long I had been out, but it was dark outside, only a sliver of moonlight coming in. The floor was entirely bare, not a single snake slithering. If it weren't for the snake bite in the back of my neck, I would have wondered if everything was a hallucination. I sat up; my clothes were drenched in sweat. It's hard to describe, but I felt this unexplainable lightness in my body and my soul. Like something heavy inside me was lifted.

CARRIE: We sat on those rocks for hours. Then four lights appeared on the horizon. When they got closer, I breathed a sigh of relief. Angel Asher was headed toward me on a jet ski, bouncing up and down on the waves. I still love that picture—the shot of me behind her on the ski, my hair blowing wildly in the wind, the flash catching half of my face and her back. The internet went nuts for that photo.

When we got to shore, I realized that the rest of the jet skis had gone separate ways. It was just Angel and me alone on the beach. The leaderboard was now a four-way dead heat. Kiana was on top, followed by Nicki Mo. I was close behind in third and Andrea was fourth.

I took out my phone and inspected the beach for survivors. There was nothing left. Just scattered debris of surfboards and the imprint of what appeared to be bodies dragged through the sand. I checked on everyone's profiles, but no one had posted. Angel came back with a pile of driftwood and quickly made us a fire. We sat in silence as she stared at me through the flames.

AUDIO FROM 'II' ACCOUNT:
CARRIE: Can I ask you something. Do you ever think about that day I beat you?
ANGEL: [LAUGHS] That was a long time ago.
CARRIE: It probably meant more for me than it did you. But I always wonder what would have happened if you'd beat me.
ANGEL: I don't follow.
CARRIE: After I won that event, my brother took my training to another level. He became obsessed. Deep down, I think he was scared he was going to screw things up like everything else in his life. That's why he took me to surf Half Moon Bay. I wasn't ready. The conditions were dangerous. I shouldn't have been in the water. **[STARES IN THE FIRE]** So I always wondered if I had lost… maybe he wouldn't have pushed so hard. He might not have taken me that day. And if I hadn't

gotten hurt, he might have had a reason to stay sober.

ANGEL: But you did beat me. And he is gone. **[PAUSES]** You know that day wasn't the first time our paths crossed.

CARRIE: Really?

ANGEL: When we were in fifth grade, our schools arranged a surf day together. **[SMILES]** When I saw you surf, I knew you were going to be the best in the world. The only girl talented enough to beat me.

CARRIE: How did Tuck end up training you?

ANGEL: **[POKING FIRE WITH STICK]** I went on a losing streak after my loss to you. I was searching for an edge, a new trainer. Your brother was one of the best.

CARRIE: So what happened?

ANGEL: He was using heavily at that time. He wasn't reliable. Stopped showing up to our sessions.

CARRIE: Is he still alive?

ANGEL: What do you mean?

CARRIE: This whole thing. These mysterious clues I've been getting. It feels like he's on the island with me. Watching me. Guiding me.

ANGEL: **[SMILES]** Well, there's only one way to find out.

[ANGEL POURS A CUP OF TEA FROM A THERMOS] To enter the next challenge, you must go through an initiation.

[ANGEL HANDS CARRIE THE TEA]

CARRIE: What is it?

ANGEL: Snake venom, or as Wyatt's lackeys like to call it, fear serum.

CAL: After leaving the shack, I scrambled through the jungle trying to find my way back to the beach. I had no idea where Carrie was, but I figured the beach was a good place to start. I walked for hours until I spotted a cloud of smoke rising above the canopy. When I got closer, I realized that the smoke wasn't coming from a small campfire but a huge swell of flames. From the perimeter of the beach, I got a clear look at the horrifying ceremony before me.

CARRIE: The tea tasted like rainwater and dirt, and the effects were instant. This tingling sensation running up and down my spine, numbing the pain in my legs. At first it was warm and light, this beautiful glow. But deep down, I felt something else. All my inner shit rising to the surface.

ANGEL: Tell me about that tattoo. Tuck had one just like it.
CARRIE: It's kind of a fucked-up story.
ANGEL: Where else do we have to be?
CARRIE: It was my brother's favorite book... Alice's Adventures in Wonderland. He said that within the story was the key to life. That everyone must go down their own personal rabbit hole. My injury was my rabbit hole. No one thought I could recover from that knee injury.

Except for him.

He was subtle at first, leaving surf magazines on my bed, turning on old surf movies before I'd walk into the room. Then it was tough love. Calling me a quitter. But then he tried a different tactic... About ten months after the accident, he brought a bottle of tequila and got me shitfaced. Then he waited until I passed out and carried me to the beach. When I woke up, he was standing there in a wetsuit. I was still too hungover and injured to surf, but I paddled out with him at sunrise. That afternoon, we went to the tattoo shop and got tattoos. He told me that the Cheshire cat was a reminder that he would be with me on my journey. Always there for me. And his tattoo, the outline of Alice, was his…

Wait did you see that?

LANE: I was watching the live video from the 'II' channel. Halfway through her story, Carrie just stopped talking. Her pupils were the size of golf balls. The drugs were kicking in. I was like . . . Oh shit, here we go.

CARRIE: I know I was hallucinating, but it was so clear. A wispy, shadowy thing scampering across the beach. I stared out into the darkness. The drugs turned on me. My pulse pounded from every part of my body. I could feel it in my eyelids, my elbows. My vision went next. Angel's face swelled and shifted back and forth, her eyes transforming into the dark eyes of Wyatt James. I needed to get away from her. I turned to the jungle, and lo and behold, the silvery figure materialized again. I swear it was a Cheshire Cat begging me to follow him. Some sort of incarnation of my brother. I knew it was just the drugs. But I wanted to believe it was really him.

LANE: Oh, she was tripping balls.

CAL: Back at the beach, I found the source of the flames—an inexplicable ceremony, a circle of cloaked men with ski masks, surrounding a disfigured body, who sat unmoving in a chair next to the fire, his eye sockets hallowed out. It was one of the contestants, Dan. In front of him, a canvas propped on an easel. In the glow of the firelight, Wyatt James emerged from the circle, taking his place in front of the canvas. All I felt was rage.

CARRIE: And then I was running, chasing this hallucination of my brother deeper into the jungle. I swatted away the thick branches that were slicing through my flesh. As I ran, Tuck's voice echoed from all sides, whispering my name. Somewhere along the way, I ate shit, crashing down into a muddy puddle. When I looked up, the Cheshire Cat was staring down at me from a tree. I know this sounds crazy, but I swear, it was Tuck's smile. That wide, playful grin I loved so much.

CAL: Shaking with anger, I watched Wyatt in the glow of the fire. A ghost I'd been chasing my entire life. His brushstrokes were fast and wild, like a mad conductor of an orchestra. The masked men around him kept chanting, *"undecim, undecim,"* over and over, their voices quickening with Wyatt's brushstrokes.

What did it mean?

It means "eleven" in Latin.

Then Wyatt pulled his hand away and the voices stopped. A masked man took the canvas, and the circle disbanded. They all shuffled away from the beach. That's when I decided to confront my father's killer.

CARRIE: The cat jumped down to a lower branch, so I was face to face with Tuck's warm blue eyes. Then he started talking to me. His voice is still so clear in my mind. "You gave up…"

I gave up… **[SNICKERS, TAKES DEEP BREATH]**

My comeback was the hardest thing I ever had to do. But I stared at this tattoo every day, and I recommitted. Because my brother believed in me, even when no one else did. I loved having a sense of purpose. I loved getting stronger. There was this date on my calendar that I stared at each day. A small event, nothing big. Just a local surf competition. But that was enough.

On the eve of the event, I wanted to re-watch surf videos with Tuck, but he didn't come home that night. Nor was he there when I woke up in the morning. But I knew he would meet me at the beach. He wouldn't let me down. He was my big brother.

But he never showed. The next few moments happened in slow motion. Kiana sprinting down the beach, holding her phone in the air. My heart beating wildly as I dropped my board, running toward her just as the air horn blew for the start of the heat.

I sat by Tuck's bedside, holding his hand, crying, punching him in the arm for abandoning me. This was the first time he'd over-dosed. His addiction intensified after my accident. I told him that I wasn't going to surf again. Not until he got clean.

Well, the joke's on me because my brother never got clean. I spent the next few years dropping him off and picking him up from rehab. Searching for him all over Los Angeles...I never surfed again. I guess we both kept our promises.

And seeing that cat, or that fucking hallucination, I just lost my shit. I lost my shit with the whole world watching.

AUDIO FROM 'II' ACCOUNT: You broke your fucking promise! You said you wouldn't give up on me. You left me. You abandoned me!

CARRIE: And you know what that fucking hallucination said to me, "I'm sorry, Carrie. I'm sorry." **[WIPING TEARS]** And then his final words: "You need to find out what happened to me. Whatever it takes. Be the fearless girl that I know you are."

CAL: I ran to Dan's mutilated body slumped in the chair, the fire still burning. A gunshot wound was visible on his bare chest. He was dead. I stared through the flames at the concealed face of Wyatt James and I screamed, "You're a monster! What did you do to my father?"

That mechanical, dark voice boomed. "I gave him the death he desired."

"No! You murdered him," I said. "Just like you're going to do with all these contestants. What are you planning for Carrie?"

Wyatt stood there for several painful minutes before speaking. "They must all atone for their sins."

"You're a fucking madman," I yelled.

Wyatt glanced at Dan before stepping closer to me, so close that I could see the black stenciled symbols on his mangled ski mask, including, XIIX.

"Do you know why God put evil in the Garden of Eden?" he asked. "To expose the shadows of man. For only after darkness was emancipated could true restoration and healing begin. The only way to salvation is through the darkness, my child. Your father understood what it took to move humanity forward. One tainted soul means nothing on the grand scale."

"Who was my father to you?" I demanded.

"Keep seeking," Wyatt whispered. And then something heavy struck the back of my head and everything went dark.

CARRIE: I don't remember much after the hallucination. It was like falling into a black hole, and having nothing solid to grasp ahold of. The next thing I know, sunlight and a blurry figure were staring down at me. Then a familiar southern accent booming in my ear. "Good morning, darlin'."

Nicki Mo's face came into focus. She was standing over me with a knife in her hand. Despite being completely disorientated, I scrambled backward, my eyes glued to the sharp blade. But Nicki Mo just smiled, throwing the knife back into her hip holster.

AUDIO FROM 'II' ACCOUNT [NICKI MO]: Jesus, surfer girl. Why so jumpy?

CARRIE: The night wasn't easy to piece together. Based on the footage, I had gone live, running through the jungle with the camera under my nose like some indie horror movie. Nicki Mo filled in the gaps while she sharpened her knives.

AUDIO FROM 'II' ACCOUNT [NICKI MO]: Well darlin', you were screaming bloody murder. I would have left you to die if it weren't for Angel and your fans begging me to come rescue you. It's not in my nature to save a scraggily little girl running through the jungle on drugs, but I made an exception.

CARRIE: Then she smiled, plunging the knife into the ground and said. . .

AUDIO FROM 'II' ACCOUNT [NICKI MO]: But I ain't gonna save you next time.

CAL: I awoke to the smell of eggs on a frying pan. I reached to the back of my head to find a softball-sized knot. Angel Asher was cooking in sweatpants and an oversized t-shirt. To the right of us were the charred remains of the bonfire, including the chair where Dan's corpse had been.

AUDIO FROM UNAIRED 'II' FOOTAGE:
[FIRE CRACKLING IN THE BACKGROUND]
ANGEL: He's gone.
CAL: Where?
ANGEL: He doesn't tell us his comings and goings.

CAL: Does he plan on killing them off one
by one?
ANGEL: What did you expect? They were all
going to collect some prize money and be sent
home on private jets?
CAL: Where's Carrie?
ANGEL: She's onto the next challenge.**[SMILING]**
So have you figured it out? How everyone's all
connected?
CAL: Everyone here knew Tuck.
ANGEL: Getting warmer.
CAL: What about you?
ANGEL: We all came to the island to purge
something. Including you. Wyatt left this.
[HOLDS OUT ENVELOPE]

CAL: With Angel's curious eyes staring at me, I opened the envelope from Wyatt. It was the next pages of my father's logs.

ENTRY 4: I will paint my masterpiece on the island's highest summit,
Satan's Peak, named for the jagged boulders that resemble the devil's
horns. The demons that live on this island reside in a small cave at the
top of the mountain. This is where my final ceremony will take place.

As soon as I was done reading, I looked up at the mountain. Sure
enough, two long pointy rocks protruded outward. My father's
final steps were in front of me. Before I made my decision, I asked
Angel, "What about Carrie?"

AUDIO FROM UNAIRED 'II' FOOTAGE:
ANGEL: She needs to find out why she's here.
What we're all doing here. She's the only one
who can save us.

CARRIE: After I got the recap from Nicki Mo, I should have ventured out on my own. But she invited me to stay and help myself to her food and water. After the drug trip, it was too tempting to pass up. Nicki Mo had made quite a little camp for herself, fastening a shelter out of old tarps. I was desperate to forget the hallucination of my brother. I was stupid to believe that Tuck was still alive. Tuck made me vulnerable. I needed to be strong.

Over the next few hours, I did my best to clean myself up, wiping off the grime and mud, and pulling up my hair. I checked in on Kiana. Her tribute song from the rock was trending, but she hadn't posted anything since yesterday, nor was her footage broadcasted on the 'II' account. I wondered if she had survived whatever shit Wyatt put her through. As the sun began to set, Nicki Mo made a roaring fire and was cooking a pig that she hunted. She asked me to join her. As I was digging into the meat, I noticed her watchful gaze.

AUDIO FROM 'II' ACCOUNT:
NICKI MO: Did they give you the snake venom too?
[CARRIE NODS]
NICKI MO: What did you see?
CARRIE: Nothing. Just darkness.
NICKI MO: You know what I saw? An old hunting shack my father used to take me to. He let me drink beer while I watched him skin the animals that he shot. He wanted a son... But you know, I guess I was the next best thing.
[NICKI MO SQUINTS]
NICKI MO: I saw your little outburst on the rock. Saw all the photos people have been posting about your brother. Know what's funny, I think I've seen him before. On the night he disappeared.

CARRIE: It took me a second to register her confession. When I glanced up, our phones buzzed with notifications. The next challenge was posted but Nicki Mo didn't even look at her phone. She kept watching me with bloodthirsty eyes.

CAL: The hike to Satan's Peak was excruciating. I followed this steep, narrow, overgrown path to the top of the mountain. With each step, I thought about my father. What had he come on this island to make peace with? How had he been so sure he was going to die?

AUDIO FROM 'II ACCOUNT [KAYLYN JENSON]: Hello, Carrie and Nicki Mo. Congratulations on finding each other in paradise. In the next challenge, you will be going head-to-head, which means only one of you will advance. The contestant who gets the most likes on their next post will get a challenge designed specifically for them, as well as a leg up on their opponent. Good luck. And as always, may fame and followers be upon you.

CARRIE: When I was done watching the video, I yelled at Nicki Mo. "Tell me what you know." Did she really have information about my brother? But she didn't answer me. With a smirk on her face, she dumped water on the fire and extinguished the flames. "I'll save that for another time," she said. Then, in a quick instant, she turned the camera around and snapped a picture with her two favorite knives. She tapped away on her phone, and that was that. She posted the photo.

[SHAKES HER HEAD]

You know what bothered me the most about that post? Nicki Mo might have been a redneck hillbilly, at least she knew her brand. She knew what her followers liked about her. And me? I had no idea what I was going to post. What did my fans actually like about me? My looks. My sporadic emotional outbursts. What was I going to post? I remember stopping at another picture that @HarrysPizza tagged me in. Another photo of Tuck and me in front of their store. I was only thirteen in that picture, but I was so cocky, so carefree, so fucking confident. So sure of myself. If only I had known what the next decade had in store. My brother was healthy in that picture. Still lean and thin, but his eyes were lucid, his ribs weren't showing.

I swiped away from the picture. I finally found a bikini photo from the shoot back home. Maybe I thought that was the only thing my fans cared about. But as soon as I posted, I knew I had lost the first part of the challenge. It wasn't good enough. *I* wasn't good enough.

CAL: It was dusk by the time I made it to the top of the mountain. I was panting in exhaustion, soaked in sweat, staring out beyond the horned rocks that extended through a heavy mist. But there was no cave to be found. On the ground was a circular pile of lava rocks with a dried-up snakeskin in the middle. Then I reread the final page of my father's log.

ENTRY 5: At midnight, my apprentice assisted me in the ceremony. I stood atop hot lava rocks. The snake's lethal fangs plunged deep into my flesh. The venom circulate in my veins, rumbling the darkness from within. The monster awakened. My regrets. My sadness. My grief. Inside the cave, I shall face the great demon. I will resurrect into a new being. I walk into the mist.

When I looked up from the page, I spotted something—mist simmering in between the lava rocks. It took me a few hours, but after moving a few boulders, the opening of the cave revealed itself. Was this the cave my father went to die?

AUDIO FROM 'II ACCOUNT [KAYLYN JENSON]:
Congratulations, Nicki Mo. You have won the first part of the challenge. The knockout

challenge will be designed for your skillset. Carrie and Nicki Mo, you will face off in a one-on-one fight to the death. The winner will advance to the next round. The loser will die famous.

JOSS: I was in disbelief when they announced the challenge. I thought, *How could this get any more gruesome?* But then came the poll—users would be voting on what weapon to give Nicki Mo as an advantage. There were ten items on that list. Everything from brass knuckles and swords to a nail gun and chicken wire. Nicki Mo's fans would select what weapon she would kill Carrie with.

CARRIE: When the video ended, Nicki Mo walked back to the firepit, still grinning as the smoke rose from the extinguished embers. She looked at me the way a predator stares at its prey. Her ultimate fantasy was coming true. This was what she came to the island for. She was going to kill me and skin me like an animal.

AUDIO FROM 'II' ACCOUNT [KAYLYN JENSON]: The votes have been tallied. Nicki Mo will be receiving a crossbow as her weapon of choice. Good luck, contestants.

CARRIE: I sat there in silence, trying to process the outcome. But time was a luxury I didn't have. Within minutes of the announcement, the robotic voice blasted through a hidden speaker in the trees.

AUDIO FROM 'II' ACCOUNT: The challenge will begin in three, two, one.

CAL: The tunnel was cold and misty, like it had a breath of its own. I tiptoed through the darkness. Call me crazy, but I could feel something evil in that cave. That shadowy vibrational energy my father spoke about. The same one that ran through my veins after the snake bite. Finally, the tunnel opened, and I shined my cell phone light across a dark cavern. Charred remains of easels and canvases were scattered about. I knew instantly. This was my father's work. But what happened to all these paintings?

CARRIE: When the challenge buzzer sounded, I didn't hesitate—I dashed into the jungle without a direction or destination in mind. My plan was to get as far away from Nicki Mo as possible. But there was just one little problem. The wound on my calf opened and blood was streaming down my leg. I must have been less than a mile from Nicki Mo's camp when my body gave out, and I keeled over in exhaustion. The only thing left to do was hide. I scrambled behind a tree and did my best to stay quiet.

JOSS: Nicki Mo gave Carrie quite a head start while she got acquainted with her new crossbow. She was putting on a show for her fans.

LANE: It was disgusting the way Nicki Mo tracked her, the way she followed the blood, the scent, everything. At one point, Nicki Mo went live, staring right into the camera.

AUDIO FROM NICKI MO'S ACCOUNT: [WHISPERS]
Hello, y'all. As you know, I've been asked to hunt down surfer girl. To be honest, I wish she made this a little more difficult. I do hate hunting injured animals. Plus, all that privilege leaves quite the scent. **[HOLDS FINGER TO HER LIPS]** Shhhhh. Looks like she's right around the corner. I'm sure she's shaking in her boots. Should we finish her off? Give me a thumbs up if you agree.

JOSS: The little hearts and thumbs up emojis were flying on Nicki Mo's account. Her fans wanted Carrie's head on a spike.

CARRIE: My breath hitched when I saw Nicki Mo saunter into the clearing, crossbow in hand. I was shaking, trying desperately to remain quiet. But she knew.

AUDIO FROM 'II' ACCOUNT [NICKI MO]: Come out, come out, wherever you are.

CARRIE: My only chance was to make a run for it. I counted in my head, *one, two, three…*

CAL: On the floor of the cave were at least fifteen charred paintings. Most of the canvases were burnt to a crisp, but you could make out a nose here, a smile there. They looked oddly familiar. I had seen these before . . . They were similar to the portraits of my father from Wyatt's installation. As I inspected more closely, I noticed three unique pieces that survived. They were painted on the cave wall.

The first: A portrait of my mother as a young woman. The words "My love" were painted underneath. My father captured her face perfectly, her soft skin, her black hair, and even more startling, her hazel eyes. It was the first time seeing him paint anyone's eyes. The next painting was a portrait of me as a child. He made my face long and thin, my ears abnormally large. As if his mind couldn't piece together my face from memory. But he painted my green eyes. Those were spot on. He knew my eyes.

When I got to the third one, my insides shook with anger. He painted the masked face of Wyatt James, with his dark, black eyes behind the ski mask.

As soon as I put my hand to the painting, a gust of mist overtook the cave, and fear slithered down my spine. The dark vibrations returned, and with it, I felt my father's presence. I sensed what happened in the cave. The evidence was right in front of me.

CARRIE: The arrow went straight into my injured calf. The pain was like nothing I'd experienced. The metal sliced even deeper through the already tender layers of flesh, so deep that I could feel the metal on my bone. I was on my knees, screaming in agony. Then I reached for the arrow and ripped it out. The blood poured down my leg as I collapsed to the ground. I've never felt pain like that. I crawled to a nearby tree, hiding behind the trunk.

AUDIO FROM 'II' ACCOUNT [NICKI MO]: Ooooo —that one must have hurt. **[RELOADS CROSSBOW, TIPTOES FORWARD]** Why don't you come on out and we can end this little hunt? What's it going to take? How about I tell you how I knew your brother? **[RAISES EYEBROWS]**

That got your attention, didn't it? I was there at Wonderland that night, looking to let loose. So I asked around about getting some drugs, and sure enough, your brother turned out to be quite the little dealer. Good looking man, wasn't he? By now, you must be wondering what all of us have in common. It took me a while to piece it together.

But some of these faces looked so familiar, including your little bestie, Kiana. We were flying to the island when it finally clicked. I saw her that night. She was fighting with your brother. It was quite the heated argument. I wonder if she knows something about his disappearance.

CARRIE: When she said it, it was almost like the pain and fear left my body. In its place, pure, unfiltered rage. Did Kiana really know what happened to Tuck? Could she really have something to do with his disappearance? The hallucination of my brother appeared so clearly in my mind. *You need to find out what happened* *to me. Be the fearless girl I know you are.* And in his words, I found purpose. I *was* here for a reason. The answers to my brother's disappearance were on this island. I wiped my tears and stood up. It was time to stop hiding.

LANE: And then Carrie limped out into the clearing.

JOSS: Everyone started screaming at the projector, "No. No. No."

AUDIO FROM 'II' ACCOUNT [NICKI MO]: An honorable exit.

LANE: What Carrie said next made her legendary.

AUDIO FROM 'II' ACCOUNT [CARRIE ANDREWS]: If you want to win, you'll need to shoot me in the fucking head.

CAL: My father's final moments came to me in a flash. I pictured him painting the portraits in a state of madness. The poison must have been too strong, the demons too overwhelming. And as he painted on the cave wall, he turned and saw the silhouette of a man at the entrance. It was Wyatt James. He was there to kill my father.

LANE: We all watched Carrie walk straight up to Nicki Mo, until they were face to face. But Nicki Mo didn't budge. She just kept smiling, the crossbow pointed right at Carries head. Would she really execute Carrie at point blank in front of millions of spectators?

AUDIO FROM 'II' ACCOUNT:
NICKI MO: You got guts, surfer girl, I'll give you that. Any final words?
CARRIE: You want to know one of the first things my brother taught me?
NICKI MO: What's that?

CARRIE: A wave doesn't care about your intentions. It won't give you a break or play games with you. So, if you hesitate even in the slightest, you've already lost.
NICKI MO: Get to the point.
CARRIE: That's a mistake that you just made.

JOSS: Then one of the BlueLA employees yells, "Look, look." They spotted Carrie fumbling with something behind her back.

LANE: In a quick instant, Carrie thrust a knife into Nicki Mo's ribcage.

JOSS: Nicki Mo fell backward in shock. But she wasn't going down without a fight.

CARRIE: We were both injured, but Nicki Mo was strong. Much stronger than me. She tackled me to the ground, and my head exploded in pain. She was choking me, clasping my neck tighter and tighter, that evil smirk on her face. As she choked me, she leaned in and whispered through gritted teeth, "Your brother is fucking dead."

LANE: Suddenly, the two rolled out of the camera frame. Viewers couldn't see what happened next.

CARRIE: She nearly choked me to death. But the words kept rattling over and over in my head. *Find out what happened to me.* There was no way I was dying without the truth. My free hand scrambled for something, anything. I grabbed a jagged rock and swung with all my might. With all the anger festering inside me. *Fuck everyone who ever doubted me. Fuck all these people for lying to me.* I struck her right on her temple, and her hands released from my neck.

LANE: All viewers saw was a lifeless hand in the frame. The Redditors quickly dissected the screenshot, and concluded that the hand belonged to Nicki Mo. But no one knew if she was dead or unconscious. When the 'II' camera finally cut back to Carrie, she was crying with blood all over her hands.

AGENT COOPER: One of my agents threw up when he found Nicki Mo's corpse. Her face looked like tenderized meat. That was the moment Carrie lost her sanity. That was the moment she became a killer. And Nicki Mo wouldn't be her last victim.

CARRIE: I'll tell you what I told the FBI. I don't remember hitting her a second time with the rock. Maybe wild animals got to the corpse.

CAL: As the images swirled in my head, I noticed a single charred match on the ground. Wyatt James had set fire to the cave. He walked forward, through the flames. My dad, lost in his state of madness, had turned to run away. His footprints were right in front of me, still etched in the black sand after all these years. He ran through a tunnel in the back of the cave.

Retracing his footsteps, I emerged out the other side. As I stood on the edge of the cliff, with the sun setting in the background, I knew how my father died. Wyatt James cornered him. He pushed him to the edge, and then off this cliff. Was he jealous of my father? Did the apprentice outgrow the master? From the top of the mountain, I could see the far end of the island, a tall lighthouse perched on the cliff. Instinctively, I knew. The finale would take place there. That was where I would face my father's killer.

EPISODE NINE:

THE FINALE

CARRIE: Still gasping for air, I glanced over at Nicki Mo's lifeless body, the blood pooling out of her ear. I was in shock. I killed someone with my own hands. *I killed someone.* I kept mumbling it over and over until finally I broke. Could you blame me? The weight of the last few days crashed down. I hadn't slept in days. But I wasn't sorry for what I did. I defended myself. I did what needed to be done. Out of habit, and maybe to escape reality, I reached for my phone, and I just scrolled, my hands still covered in her blood. I was now at 7.9 million followers. I had a range of notifications, mostly fans congratulating me. As if I should be praised for the things I did. But there was a message that caught my eye. A video message from Kiana.

AUDIO FROM KIANA'S MESSAGE:
Hello, Carrie. If you're watching this, it means we are the last two contestants left. By now, you know that I attended Wonderland on the night Tuck disappeared. You must also know that I've been hiding secrets from you. Maybe it's time we had a little face to face. You can find me back where this all started.

CARRIE: Physically, I was a mess. My leg was injured badly. I was covered in blood. But there was nothing that could have stopped me. I hobbled to the beach cove just as night fell.

There was an eerie feeling to the place. Trashcans filled with smoke and rising ash. Tin roofing from the tiki bars flapping in the wind. Red solo cups blowing around the sand like tumbleweeds. The glitz and glamour of that first night washed away.

Kiana greeted me on the beach. It seemed like years since we were dancing right in that very spot, surrounded by our favorite influencers. A lot changed since then. We both had done things. Seen things. Unlike me, she still looked put together. She sported a spotless crop top and a pair of biker shorts; her hair tied up in a top knot. She didn't acknowledge the blood on my clothes. She knew what I did. Instead, she passed me a bottle of tequila, "Looks like we could both use a drink."

And that was it. We just stood there, passing the bottle back and forth.

AUDIO FROM 'II' ACCOUNT:
KIANA: What did you see when they gave you the snake venom?
CARRIE: My brother. And you?
KIANA: I saw you, Carrie. . . Well, not you exactly. It was an evil version of you. A demonic version. You were trying to kill me.

CARRIE: Then she took a deep swig, a small smile twisting in the corner of her mouth as a notification appeared on our phones.

AUDIO FROM 'II' ACCOUNT [KAYLYN JENSON]:
Welcome, Kiana and Carrie to the final showdown—The Bad Blood Challenge. In this challenge, you'll once again have to answer the question: How far would you be willing to go

for fame and followers? Secrets between
friends must be uncovered.

At the conclusion of this announcement, the
Influencer Island feed will go offline. No
audio or video will be broadcasted. Which
means what happens on the beach, stays on the
beach. Both of you must remain inside the
boundaries. There are guards at every exit to
ensure you adhere to these rules. Your goal is
simple: Destroy the competition. Neither of
you can leave until the other is dead.

JOSS: And then the feed went dark.

CARRIE: Neither of us reacted to the video. This type of shit was
our new normal. As promised, five masked guards lined up at the
edge of the jungle, holding AK-47s. There was nowhere to go.
Nowhere to hide. There was no other option but to kill my best
friend. We passed the tequila bottle back and forth, until the last
swig was taken. Then Kiana told me she was going to go clear her
head. But before she left, she looked back and said, "I was your
friend once, Carrie. Just know that." Then she walked away.

Before the showdown, I walked to the shoreline, letting my toes
sink into the wet sand. I spoke to my brother. I knew he brought
me here for a reason. He needed me to uncover everything, even
Kiana's secrets. And the only way to do that was to get to the end.
At midnight, an hour into the challenge, I walked onto the dance
floor, a circular area surrounded by burning tiki torches whipping
in the wind. Shortly after, Kiana came to face me.

CARRIE: You drugged me that first night,
didn't you?
KIANA:[NODDING] With a little help from my
mentor.

CARRIE: So that's it. All our years of friendship.

KIANA: Years of friendship…

[KIANA PACES AROUND CARRIE]

You never saw it, did you? It happened under your nose the entire time. I've been in love with Tuck since we were kids. It took him a while to come around, but when he did, he was mine.

[CARRIE CLENCHES JAW]

KIANA: Sometimes, I thought you figured it out. But I underestimated how self-absorbed you could be. We fucked every chance we could get. Sometimes, you were even in the other room when it happened. I loved everything about Tuck. How he touched me. How he tasted. Of course, he forbid me from telling you. He was so worried about his precious sister being mad at him… So worried about losing you.

CARRIE: Why were you at Wonderland?

KIANA: That night was particularly special. You see, I had given Tuck an ultimatum. Come clean to your sister or I walk. I was tired of living in the shadows. So we made plans the next day to tell you. We were even going to take an extended trip after. But first, Tuck needed to sell the last of his drugs. It was the only way he could make a clean break. But that night, we got into a fight. He chickened out. He decided he'd rather lose me than risk telling you. Do you know how hard it is to love someone who only has room for one woman in his life? How hard it was to watch him become a full-blown addict because I wasn't enough? Because he felt guilty for ruining

your stupid career. I could never compete
with you.

CARRIE: What happened to him?

KIANA: Isn't that the million-dollar question?
You see, I came to this island for answers
too, Carrie. I came to find your brother.

CARRIE: He's not dead, is he?

KIANA: I've suspected it for a while now. That
he sent us here for a reason. How else would
Wyatt have known to put my invitation on the
lifeguard tower? That was the first place I
had sex with Tuck. He snuck out of your apartment to meet me. After we made love, he tried
to end things. He told me that it wasn't
right. That we should be ashamed of ourselves.
But I'm tired of being ashamed.

CARRIE: Fuck you, Kiana.

KIANA: [PULLS OUT A GUN FROM HER WAISTBAND]
I'm sorry, Carrie. But only one of us is going
to find out if Tuck is at the end of all this.
And this time, he's going to be all mine.

[KIANA COCKS BACK GUN HAMMER]

CARRIE: You're going to shoot me in cold blood.

KIANA: You wouldn't be the first.

CARRIE: What have you become?

KIANA: I'll admit, when I saw the gun in the
backpack on the rock, I wondered if I could do
it. But then I saw Dan pathetically crawling
up the rock, and I decided to put him out of
his misery. Thankfully, my mentor kept the
footage off the internet. Now shooting Andrea
point blank was a little harder. But she had
the unaired footage that could ruin me. My
fans wouldn't understand.

CARRIE: You're a murderer.

KIANA: Tuck gave me some advice a long time ago that I didn't take. He told me to stop playing small. To take what I want in life. The sheep, the ignorant masses, they don't want to see a starving artist. They want to see a winner. They want to be let in on the fantasy. All of them, sitting at their useless jobs, living their pointless existences. I used to be weak. Letting everyone push me around. Letting you push me around. Letting my manager fuck me over. So I decided to play things differently. Oh, don't look at me like that. What about Trevor and Nicki Mo?

CARRIE: It was self-defense.

KIANA: Don't pretend that you don't love it. We are larger than fucking life. Famous beyond our wildest dreams. When this is all over, the world will be open to me. Imagine the sold-out shows I'm going to play. With Tuck right by my side. Any last words?

CARRIE: [LIMPING FORWARD, UNFAZED] Smile for the camera, you murderous bitch.

KIANA: What are you talking about?

CARRIE: The challenge wasn't to physically kill you; it was to symbolically kill you. Or did you forget what this competition is all about? I wanted the world to really see who you are.

KIANA: What the fuck are you talking about?

CARRIE: You see, there's one little thing you forgot, one rule of being an influencer. . .

[KIANA GRABS HER PHONE. THE GUN SHAKES IN HER HAND.]

CARRIE: Someone is always watching. Say "hi" to the fans at home, Kiana.
[CARRIE POINTS TO THE PHONE HIDDEN INSIDE THE PALM LEAVES COVERING THE BAR]

CARRIE: Kiana began firing the gun at the phone. But the damage was done. Two masked men disarmed her, pinning her to the ground. I grabbed her phone, turning it so she could see the screen. It was a thing of beauty watching her fans turn on her. More importantly, I won Influencer Island. **[PAUSES]** Or so I thought.

BELLA ALLESANDRA: As soon as I realized the outcome, I tried to escape the war room, but Wyatt's goons apprehended me. Where did the masked men take me and Kiana? **[TAKES A DEEP BREATH]** Where all the rest of them went to die. The hole of fucking despair.

CAL: On my way down the mountain, I stumbled into a clearing to find Nicki Mo's body in a pool of blood. Her phone was still next to her. When I logged into her Gl!tch, I went straight to Carrie's profile. I knew what was coming next. I didn't have much time to save her. I knew who the mysterious contestant was.

CARRIE: I should have slept, but the adrenaline was egging me onward. More than that, I knew if I stopped, if I took one moment to process everything, I would break. I needed to keep moving. I needed to know what happened to my brother. Why Wyatt brought me to that island. Angel messaged me directions to the lighthouse where the finale would take place. It was a two-mile trek down the beach. When I got there, the sun was just coming up, illuminating a gorgeous old lighthouse perched on top of the cliff. Before I took the trail to the top, I saw my mentor, Angel, walking from the opposite direction. She was in a contest-branded gold bikini, a surfboard under her arms.

I asked Angel, "Where's Wyatt?"

She pointed at the lighthouse. "Up there," she said, holding her hand out to me. And I'll admit, there was a sense of relief when our fingers interlaced. Like all the horror and bullshit was over. She helped me survive, and I was thankful.

Angel said that they were preparing for the finale. She asked if I'd like to paddle out with her one last time before I discovered the truth. She smiled when she saw my leg. "Just paddle out with me," she said, pointing to a second surfboard and a gold bathing suit near the shore. "I'll tell you everything you want to know before confronting Wyatt James in front of millions of people."

I agreed.

It was one of the most beautiful sunrises. The waves were perfect that morning. And for a second, I stopped thinking about what I'd done. It was a temporary escape. That was something the water always gave me. It cleansed me. There was something so calming about rocking back and forth on the board, in tune with the sea's energy. Angel and I sat up on our boards, taking in the horizon.

Finally, I asked, "What do you know about him?"

JOSS: What you're about to hear is unaired audio taken from a microphone implanted in Angel's surfboard.

```
UNAIRED AUDIO FROM 'II': [WAVES LAPPING]
ANGEL: I'm sure Wyatt is going to tell you why
he brought you to the island. Honestly, I've
been thinking about that question since the
beginning. What did Wyatt know about that
night at Wonderland? What did he know about
your brother?
CARRIE: You were there?
ANGEL: Of course… We all were.
CARRIE: But—
ANGEL: Just listen. I want you to think long
and hard about that day our schools met at the
beach to surf. Do you remember what you and
your friends called us kids from Santa Ana?
CARRIE: Angel—
ANGEL: Trailer Trash. So lesser, that you
wouldn't even surf the same waves as us. You
didn't want our dirt and grime rubbing off on
you. Just because we weren't born into money.
I wasn't lying about my first impression of
```

you though… How I thought you were the best surfer in the world. You were. But I made up my mind that day. I would do everything in my power to beat you. It became an obsession. I trained every free second I could, until we finally squared off at the US Open of Surfing. And all that training still wasn't enough to beat you.

Your brother caught me staring at you hoisting the trophy, with that crowd of admirers cheering and screaming your name. And I'll never forget what he said: "Buck up, Ash. You'll get used to coming in second." So you can imagine that when you got injured, I didn't shed a tear. I wanted everything you had. Including your trainer.

CARRIE: What are you talking about?

ANGEL: Days after your accident, I contacted Tuck and asked him to train me for the next US Open. I wanted you to know that I stole your trainer. He was reluctant at first. But eventually, he relented. It was the only thing he was ever good at. The only thing that made him an honest man. Kept him on the wagon. And now that his star prodigy was wallowing, he had nothing left. I knew he felt guilty, but I paid him, and he needed it to buy drugs after your father cut him off. We even fucked on the night before the competition.

When he woke up in the morning, I could tell the guilt was eating him alive. Not only did he cheat on your best friend, but he betrayed his sister by sleeping with the enemy. He left

my house in a hurry, and I wasn't sure he
would show. But he did. He came to the competition completely loaded. And right before I
ran out into the water for my first heat, he
whispered in my ear: "You'll always be a
lesser version of my sister."

I know why he did it. He was still trying to
protect you. You were his pride and joy and
helping me win was the ultimate betrayal.

After that day, I never won a competition
again. Years later, after all the sponsors,
all the followers, I thought that feeling
would go away. But it never did. Tuck's words
stayed on a loop inside my head. Somehow, I
was always chasing you. You were the ghost I
could never get rid of.

And then I saw him. That night at Wonderland,
selling drugs like the loser he was. It was
fate. He was wiry and pale, strung out. I'll
admit, I wasn't in the best headspace. They
don't tell you how lonely it can be at the
top, despite all the praise and adoration. And
when I saw him, I wanted him to hurt the way
he hurt me. So I confronted him. I told him he
was a druggie loser and that you were just
some washed up waitress that never amounted to
shit.

And you know what he said to me? Nothing. He
snickered and walked away from me. FROM ME! I
have millions of followers. I have money and
fucking fame. And still, he had the power to

hurt me. Don't you see the injustice? And as I sat back, alone in a sea of people, all I wanted to do was get rid of that feeling. I wanted to hurt you. I wanted to take the most important person away from you.

CARRIE: What the fuck did you do to my brother?

ANGEL: To tell you the truth, I didn't think I would go through with it. But when I walked into his little drug room, he looked up and rolled his eyes, and said, "Oh Jesus, what the fuck do you want?"

CARRIE: What did you do?!

ANGEL: This.

CARRIE: The knife went straight into the side of my ribs. I was in absolute shock, staring back at the eyes of my brother's killer. Soaked in pain, I fell off my board, holding my side as the blood gushed out of my body. Angel smiled and kept talking as I bobbed up and down in the water, scrambling to stay on my board, too weak to fight back.

ANGEL: I killed your brother.

CARRIE: I just kept mumbling, "No, no."

ANGEL: I watched him bleed out on the floor, and then I left him there to die. And yet, it didn't satisfy me. So when Wyatt James approached me with this proposition to come to the island, it was too tempting to pass up. He told me that the island would rid me of you once and for all. I just needed to help you get to the end.

CARRIE: I tried to climb back on my board, but I couldn't. The pain was too severe.

ANGEL: As I watched you over the course of this contest, my resentment and rage returned with a vengeance. I spent years building my social media presence. Years. And in less than three days, you have accumulated more followers, more adoration, more praise than I ever have. You know what people are calling me online? A less-hot version of Carrie Andrews.

Finally, it all clicked. The opportunity Wyatt gave me. A chance at redemption. You see, only one surfer girl will make it off the island. I'm the eleventh and final contestant, Carrie. And this time, I'm going to win.

CARRIE: She lunged at me with the knife out again, but this time, I grabbed her wrist and threw her off the board. Scrambling in the water, she grabbed hold of my neck and pushed me underwater, still slashing at me with the knife. With death knocking at my door, I latched onto my brother's words: *You better get used to coming in second.* I would *never* lose to Angel Asher. I found power in Tuck's faith. She *was* a lesser version of me

I fought with every last bit of energy inside me. I tried to shove her off, screaming beneath the water. But Angel didn't retreat. She kept pushing me down, further and further. She wanted to drag me into the depths of hell. She would rather drown with me than let me win.

But I wouldn't let that happen.

I sunk my teeth into her flesh, prying the knife from her grasp. With a quick thrust, I felt the blade penetrate the top of her muscly abs. The water muffled her scream, but I knew I had cut deep. I released the grip, and I swam to the surface for air, my entire left side still numb and throbbing. I don't know how I had the energy to swim to shore. I really don't.

CAL: I was staring at Nicki Mo's phone when I finally got to the beach. The 'II' live feed was still dark. Carrie and Angel were nowhere to be found.

CARRIE: I stumbled onto the sand, coughing, choking, bleeding. But even with the pain, I was determined to keep going. I saw the lighthouse on the cliff. I would drag my body to the top if I had to. I needed the truth. Why was I really here? Was my brother really dead?

JOSS: When the live feed resumed, a record breaking 20.6 million users were tuned in. The camera steadied on contestant Carrie Andrews, in her gold bikini, her sopping blonde hair. The camera zoomed in on an open gash on her right ribcage, the blood trickling down her body as she collapsed to the sand. Then, Angel Asher staggered out of the water, holding her bleeding stomach with one hand, a knife in the other. Carrie moved out of frame, but Angel kept walking up the beach, a look of determination in her eyes.

CARRIE: I heard her coming, but I was too weak to get away. I was crawling, leaving a trail of blood in the sand.

JOSS: On the screen, we saw Angel lift the knife above her head. But right before she was about to thrust it down, she was knocked back by something. We saw feet scrambling in the sand, heard shouting, then a loud thud before the screen went dark. Whatever happened in those moments was a complete mystery.

CAL: I did it. I bashed Angel over the head with the back of a fishing spear. But that didn't keep her down. That woman was possessed. Despite bleeding out her head and stomach, she staggered forward, charging at me, and tackled me to the ground. She was inches from putting the knife through my neck. And then all of a sudden, her body went limp as blood poured from her mouth. A bloody fishing spear was rammed through the middle of her chest. When I looked up, Carrie's determined blue eyes stared back.

CARRIE: I don't remember killing her. But I remember her body falling limply to the sand. Then I remember collapsing into Cal, the truth crashing down on me like a ten-foot swell. Tuck was dead. I finally knew it. He was gone. He wasn't going to be waiting for me at the end of this. I would never see him again. I grieved for the most important person in my life. I'm not sorry for killing Angel. There was only one ending for her. It was either her or me. Only one of us was leaving this island alive. And I made sure it wasn't my brother's killer.

CAL: I put my arms around Carrie and she guided me to a nearby rock, propping me against the edge. She was in bad shape. Emotionally, physically. I did my best to clean her wounds, wrapping a torn t-shirt around the gashes. My heart broke for her. It really did. She went through hell and back. She was now processing the death of her brother. And in that moment, I realized how much I cared about her. The thought of losing her. I just – for better or worse, I loved her.

CARRIE: I just wanted answers. I didn't care about anything else. I went through too much. And seeing you reminded me of the person I used to be. This island changed me. And by the look on your face that morning, it changed you as well.

CAL: I pulled Carrie to her feet, and we began our ascent to the lighthouse.

BELLA ALLESANDRA: The box... that fucking box. It was a wooden container, the size of a coffin. It smelled like earth and death. There were speakers inside. Loudspeakers, playing every single comment and message ever written on my account. The voice of my followers. **[SHAKES HEAD]** Imagine someone taking all the words of hate and adoration. The comments of every insecure, depressed, or angry user who has ever followed me or commented on a post. Every unhappy customer who was displeased with their body. Every pervert who posted a crude comment. Then you have someone animate those words. Give them life. Narrate them. And they whispered to you for hours on an endless loop, until all those voices were stuck inside of your head. Until you couldn't get rid of them.

How did that affect you?

If you think it broke me, it didn't. I wouldn't give Wyatt James the satisfaction. I was tougher than the others. They left me in that box all fucking night. Then, as the sun was coming up, I was dragged out by two men and injected with that poison.

I saw things, hallucinations. I saw my followers eating me, tearing at my flesh. Ripping out my hair, my teeth. An army of cannibals wearing my bones as souvenirs. Gruesome shit. Everything gets hazy after that. I was in this shadowland, a mysterious place between living and deceased. This barren desert with black sand, where everything you touch turned to ash. And in the sky, all you could see were flames. I remember walking, crawling through the shiny black sand, and a voice, that said, *Let go, surrender*. But I wouldn't. I would never give up. I kept crawling, fighting for my life.

And then what?

When I came to, I was blindfolded, but I could feel them dragging me away from flames. Then they threw me in the back of a vehicle. I knew Kiana was there because I could hear her sniffling.

We were taken back to camp, where a golden throne was placed in the main tent for another cultish ceremony. All these masked people stood in a line behind the throne, awaiting the presence of their master. It was our turn to be brought before the fucking king.

CAL: By the time we made it up the cliff, Carrie was almost unconscious. She assured me that she was okay, but her depleted body and pale face said otherwise. She'd lost a lot of blood. Then again, what choice did we have? There was no medical team, no hospital. We finally reached the lighthouse. Inside the hollowed-out concrete cylinder was a set of winding metal stairs to the top.

CARRIE: Every step was unbearable. Like shockwaves of pain shooting through my body. Finally, we reached this small control room with at least twenty small monitors and a large window to an open-air platform showcasing panoramic views of the sea. On the platform were two metal chairs and a blank canvas and paints.

CAL: Carrie and I exchanged nervous glances. After a long moment of silence, a voice reverberated through a speaker mounted on the wall. The machine-like voice of Wyatt James. "Please step outside, Carrie Andrews." When I went to follow her, the voice spoke again. "One at a time."

Wyatt James was watching us. I pleaded with Carrie to wait. I wanted us to stay together. But she didn't listen.

CARRIE: There was no more fight in me. I just wanted answers. I walked onto the platform and sat down in the metal chair, facing the back of the blank canvas.

CAL: The sound of footsteps on metal stairs echoed through the lighthouse. Wyatt James, along with two lackeys, stepped inside the control room. They immediately drew their weapons on me. "What are you going to do to her?" I screamed. Wyatt looked straight at me and said, "Enjoy the finale, Mr. Everett. I will be with you shortly."

CARRIE: Wyatt emerged on the platform in a hooded sweatshirt and his ski mask.

CAL: I was forced to watch the whole thing from behind the glass.

BELLA ALLESANDRA: And then he came, King James sat on his throne, smiling. He asked us if we atoned for our sins. If we removed our false masks. If so, he told us to kneel before him. To accept our roles in the Great Awakening to come. Kiana fell on her knees in two seconds flat.

[LAUGHS] And that's why she lost the fucking competition.

When I didn't kneel, Wyatt snickered. "Still so defiant," he said. "What will it take for you to denounce this evil entity that you created?" Or some dramatic bullshit like that. And I said, "I'd rather die." And he said, "Then that's how it shall be."

Then one of his henchmen handed him a big ass drill.

CARRIE: The blood poured out my makeshift bandage, dripping onto the concrete floor. Wyatt nodded to a masked servant in the corner, who came over with a burning iron rod. The hot iron seared into my flesh, and I screamed in agony.

CAL: I pounded the glass in the control room, desperate to stop it. But it was no use. I had to watch the girl that I loved tortured by the man I hated.

CARRIE: When the iron was removed, I slumped in the seat. And to be honest, I felt relieved. There was this overwhelming sense of surrender. I wasn't going to fight any longer. Wyatt just stared at me for a few minutes, as if he were taking it all in, absorbing my energy. Then one of his lackeys handed him a metal drill.

CAL: Suddenly, two monitors turned on in the control room. The word "LIVE" flashed on the bottom of the screen. I didn't know who was watching this footage. The entire world? His rich friends and benefactors?

JOSS: Out of nowhere, the 'II' account went back on. We saw Carrie Andrews sitting across from Wyatt James on a metal chair. The audio was muted. All I could think about was Ian Huckle's corpse. He was going to drill Carrie's eyes out the sockets in front of millions of viewers watching.

CARRIE: Then Wyatt motioned for the servant to bring something else out. I grimaced when I saw it. It was a painting of Tuck. His eyes were hidden behind the yellow blur, but I could see his pale, shrunken face, his cleft chin, the little scar where a piece of coral cut him while surfing on a vacation in Maui.

JOSS: With the help of Carrie's testimony, we have done our best to recreate this scene.

WYATT JAMES: Welcome to your final test, Carrie Andrews. What comes next is entirely up to you. But first, I'm sure you'd like to know the truth about why you are here.

LANE: We couldn't hear what they were saying, but we saw the tears rolling down Carrie's face.

WYATT JAMES: As you must know now, every contestant here attended Wonderland on the night of your brother's death, including me. Seeing masses of kids consuming drugs to mask their pain has always been a source of inspiration for me. I was weaving in and out of the crowd of lost souls, when I felt dark energy pulsing through the air. The energy of a creative being. An artist that was deprived of his life source. I followed that energy into that small cement room, where I found Tuck collapsed on the floor, a knife sticking out of his chest. He didn't have long to live.

I've seen many souls in this position, dying without hope, their wounds on display for me to paint. I asked him if I could capture him in his final minutes. He agreed. As I sketched his soul, I requested his final words. And with the last bit of energy he had left, he spoke about you. He said that you were the one good thing he's ever done with his life. He told me stories of you, Carrie. Intimate details. The moment he bought you your first surfboard. The story of the tattoo. He was so very proud of you. He told me his regrets. About his affair with Kiana. About the surf trip that ended your career. He'd lost considerable blood, but he just kept talking, and the story of you and your brother's relationship came to life. I was in awe of this powerful love that pushed him through his imminent death. The memory of his little sister. I've never known the love of a sibling or parent. So to experience that, well, it inspired me in ways you couldn't imagine. Then he asked me for a favor. He wanted me to save you.

CARRIE: Then Wyatt revealed the crumpled photo of Tuck and me on the day he gave me my first surfboard. Over my eyes was a small yellow blur.

WYATT: You became my subject, Carrie. I created Influencer Island based on Tuck's final wish. He wanted his sister to rediscover her true self. I designed this competition for you to go on a transformative journey, through your darkest fears and out the other side. I used all the stories your brother told me to guide you. To help you remember who you are. And this is the only way I knew how. I became Cheshire89 to remind you of your brother's faith. And you have done so well, my child. You have faced your darkness. You have shown great resolve. And now I will present you with your final test, a choice you must make.

BELLA ALLESANDRA: With the drill held to my fucking head, he beckoned the masked men to reveal their identity. And lo and behold, when the ski masks came off, all the influencers he kidnapped stared back at me. But they weren't my peers any longer. Even Olivia, Kiki, and Sienna were shells of their former selves. Their makeup was removed, their hair was shaved off, their faces hallowed. As I sat there in shock, Wyatt kept talking.

He said, "Your peers have removed their false identities. They have become my disciples."

I screamed, "Why don't you take off your mask, asshole?"

He smiled again and said, "I'll take off mine, if you take off ours."

CARRIE: I wiped the tears from my eyes, shaking as Wyatt presented my choices.

WYATT JAMES: Option one, there shall be no winner to Influencer Island. As soon as you leave this lighthouse, you shall delete your account and all the millions of followers you've accumulated. You will destroy this persona, this false brand you have created. You shall shed the skin of your former self, your history, your likes and dislikes, the things that make you crave the attention of others. You will become one of my disciples. You shall live with purpose, with real power. You will be a conduit of transformation. A light in the awakening to come.

CARRIE: "And option two?" I asked.

WYATT JAMES: Option two. You die famous **[GESTURES TO THE DRILL]** You will be declared the winner of Influencer Island. I will paint you as you are. And you shall die with your current follower count. They will remember you as Carrie Andrews, this brand, this entity, that you have created. The winner of the most talked about competition ever.

CARRIE: In that moment, with all the blood loss and lack of sleep, with all the grief and weight of the truth coming down on me, my life flashed before my eyes. Regardless of what anyone says, I didn't give a shit about the millions of followers. I didn't care about winning the competition. All I could picture was Tuck and me out on the water, watching an amazing set roll into shore. Smiling in the warm California sun. Those were the best moments of my life. I knew all the followers in the world wouldn't bring me back there. They wouldn't make me happy. I knew that. But I didn't want to lose the person my brother made me to be. Tuck sacrificed himself so I could live. He sent me on this journey to rediscover myself. So I could be *me* again. Carrie Andrews. Not some nameless person. Not some disciple of a fucking cult. He wanted me to be the confident girl he raised. I didn't go through all this shit just to give it all up.

BELLA ALLESANDRA: The electric drill began spinning in his hands as he inched forward, waiting for me to submit like all those weak girls before me. To fall to my knees. But I didn't. I looked that asshole straight in the eye and said, "I'm Bella motherfucking Allesandra. I built an empire from nothing. You'll have to kill me if you want to take that shit from me."

CARRIE: And then the words slipped out of my mouth. "I'd rather die."

CAL: As the drill started spinning in Wyatt's hands, I pounded on the glass, screaming at Carrie to retract her choice.

CARRIE: I kept waiting for something to change in me. To tell Wyatt hat I wanted to live. But nothing came. I accepted death. I was ready to see my brother.

JOSS: The live feed cut out when the drill was inches from Carrie's head.

CARRIE: And then Wyatt James said to me…

WYATT JAMES: Congratulations, Carrie Andrews. You are the winner of Influencer Island.

BELLA ALLESANDRA: The drill was inches from my eyeballs when it finally stopped. Wyatt James sat there, smiling. All he said was, "May God have mercy on your soul." Then his disciples grabbed my arms and put me back in the box. The place you found me **[SNICKERS]** Like I said, I was the only one who didn't succumb.

LANE: As soon as the live feed went dark, the world lost their minds. Every forum, every thread, every media outlet was in an uproar. The headlines read: *Online Social Media Contest Ends in Murder and Tragedy.* But how big of a tragedy was it? When Carrie Andrews went live again, she was lost in madness, claiming she did what she had to do to survive, but she wasn't a killer. Other than that, we were all left in the dark. And to make matters more insane, all the original influencer and contestant accounts, besides Carrie's and Bella's, were deleted from Gl!tch at the exact moment the feed went dark. Just gone. Vanished without a trace.

JOSS: We could only hope that one day the world would know what happened on that island. If there was anyone who could finish this story . . . Two days later, I got a call from Cal. He was alive. And he had quite the tale.

CAL: My fists were still resting on the glass in the control room of the lighthouse when Carrie got up from the metal seat outside on the platform. I was in shock. Carrie was alive. When she entered the control room, she didn't say a single word. She walked past me and down the stairs. Before I could chase her down, Wyatt's guards grabbed my arms and brought me out on to the concrete platform. They shoved me in a seat across from my father's killer.

Here's our best recreation of what transpired:

WYATT JAMES: Now it's your turn, Cal Everett. I've been waiting for this moment for a long time. **[WYATT TURNS THE BLANK CANVAS AROUND TO FACE ME]** There's a reason I never sold those paintings I made of your father. They were replications of his greatest work. Work that he burned to ashes before his death, inside the cave that you have already discovered.

CAL: "Is that why you killed him?" I snapped. "You were jealous?"

WYATT JAMES: As you read, Isaias entered a sacred ceremony by taking the island's venom. I tried to warn him of its power. Your father's mind was full of demons, and he was not strong enough to handle the effects. But before he went mad, he painted those self-portraits. Eleven of the most beautiful paintings I'd ever seen. When he was asleep, I witnessed them. They were better than anything I could have done in this lifetime.

But the next morning, when I was down at the beach, I saw smoke rising from the cave. When I reached the entrance, the smoke thickened, the flames raged. Isaias set fire to his paintings and had every intention of burning himself alongside them. I rushed through the flames, where I found him painting on the wall of the cave, lost in madness. He was depicting the most important people in his life. You and your mother were his final works of art.

The only eyes he ever painted.

I yelled at him to come with me, to leave the inferno. But his own eyes were as black as death itself. In his altered state, he thought I'd come to kill him. He sprinted out the other side of the cave to the edge of the cliff. I tiptoed through the flames, trying to talk sense into him, but Isaias refused to accept my help. He just smiled, speaking his last words: "Let go of your anger, my child. Lead them to paradise." Then he folded his hands across his chest and fell to his death.

CAL: "You're lying!" I yelled.

WYATT JAMES: I grieved Isaias for years. I loved your father as my own. He gave me something my family could never give me. A purpose. True power. Your father taught me everything I know.

CAL: "What am I doing here?" I screamed in anger.

WYATT JAMES: In your father's logs, you read that he entrusted his apprentice to bring you to the island. That responsibility was mine, and I failed. You see, I wasn't jealous of your father. I was jealous of you.

CAL: "I don't understand," I said.

WYATT JAMES: At your father's command, I attended your first art exhibit. I saw your work, your potential, and I was filled with envy. I believed if you came to the island, Isaias would abandon me, just like my own family. Therefore, I did not extend the invitation. I had no idea those next few days would be his last. And I often wonder, would he have had the strength to overcome if you were by his side? Would he have listened to *you*? So you are right. I am responsible for his death. I am responsible for taking away your one chance to meet your father, a great man. And for that, I am truly sorry.

It took me a long time to make peace with the guilt. But when I did, I decided that I must make things right. Your father wanted you here on the island so he could teach you. He wanted to pass his gifts down to you. So, his goal became my goal. I have spent years waiting for this moment. It's time for you to reclaim your inheritance.

You see, this contest wasn't just about fulfilling a dying boy's wish. For me, this contest was about you. About discovering the truth about your father. About you letting go of your anger and reconnecting with the creative force that flows inside your veins, passed down to you by your father.

CAL: At that point, I didn't know what to believe.

WYATT JAMES: And now, I will give *you* two choices. But it's not your death I am asking you to decide on; it is my own.

CAL: Wyatt James was asking me to kill him.

WYATT JAMES: The first option. My death will be simple. You push me off this lighthouse, and I will die the same way your father did. It will be an admirable death and perhaps what I deserve for my sins. It is you who will take my place. You shall become Isaias Everett's true apprentice.

CAL: "And option two?" I asked.

WYATT JAMES: You kill me symbolically. By painting me. Not the masked version. The real me. And in doing so, you will kill the artist known as Wyatt James. You will destroy this identity I created.

CAL: I sat there in silence for a long while. Inside me, something dark reared its head. And it wasn't the need to avenge my father. It was more than that. It was the desire to become Wyatt James. I should have been my father's apprentice. I should have been by his side, learning his techniques. It should have been me. And in one push, I would get my revenge. Didn't he deserve it? He stole everything from me. Even if he didn't kill my father, he was a murderer. Innocent people died because of him.

In my emotional state, I made the decision. I wanted Wyatt James dead. But just as I moved toward his chair, I felt something... This will sound nuts, but it was that buzzing in my fingertips. And I knew it was my father. Whatever part of him that lived inside me. Those vibrations passing through my body, begging me to follow in his footsteps and commit to my artistry. To pick up the paintbrush. A small voice inside me that said, *stop running*. Because that's what I had been doing for years.

In that moment, I realized that killing Wyatt James wouldn't bring me closer to my father. Only reconnecting with my creative force would. The same force Isaias Everett dedicated his life to. His true calling, for better or worse.

I reached for the paintbrush, and when I did, Wyatt James reached for his ski mask.

And when he pulled it from his face, I couldn't believe who stared back at me.

It wasn't a man. It was a freckly faced woman in her mid-to-late twenties with bright red hair and sharp green eyes. I recognized those eyes.

WYATT JAMES: Yes, I was the little girl in that TV sitcom. The daughter in the show, *Yellow Sub*. I was just a child when my greedy parents sold me off to Hollywood. Years of standing on set, dancing, smiling, and singing for the undeserving. Being shuffled from one commercial, one failed show to the next. I was a commodity, never good enough, never pretty enough. Always trying to please them. Longing to be famous. Then I would be happy.

When I got the part on that show, I thought my dream was finally fulfilled. I found something meaningful. I met a real family. A real father figure in Ian Huckle. And I was happy for the first time in my life. I still remember the day I first sketched the blur, staring at a man that I admired. It was the first and last painting I made out of love. But then it went away. Hollywood finally broke me. Robbed me of my faith in humanity.

I went to Ian's trailer one afternoon, and I discovered his true nature. I caught him assaulting a young production assistant. The girl escaped, but my soul did not. This man was just as evil as the rest of them. In my confusion, I told an assistant producer, who told his boss, who told the president of the studio. And instead of holding the culprit accountable, they canceled the show. They swept it under the rug. Scandal wasn't good for the bottom line.

They made the decision to destroy something so good, so pure, because of one sinful man. That failed pilot was the final dagger in my worthless career. I was only thirteen years old, and no one wanted me anymore. My bloodsucking manager fired me. My parents left me. And Ian Huckle, a man who I trusted, betrayed me. He was too much of a coward to face me. So, there I was, a discarded piece of trash.

It was fate that I met your father. Just like the moment he met your mother, he was wandering the streets by himself, looking for inspiration. And he found me, standing on a bridge, prepared to leave this world. That night, he pulled me down from the bridge and offered me something no one else could. He spoke of true artistry, far away from the evil bowels of Hollywood. He taught me how to shed the limits of my broken self, to lean into darkness. To pour my anger and fear into my art. To use my craft to bring about lasting change. And change is what I sought. I became his apprentice. He taught me of ancient traditions and secret orders . . .

CAL: "The symbol?" I asked. "What does it mean? Was my father a part of it?"

WYATT JAMES: Isaias no longer believed in the ways of the symbol. He did not believe the ends justified the means. He tried to warn me. But I didn't listen. I followed the symbol deeper into the shadows. I did everything they asked of me. I climbed to the highest ranks. I believed that the only way to bring humanity to greatness was to force it to face its darkness. But I'm not sure your father was proud of what I became. The monster you see today. I let the darkness consume me. So, I ask, will you release me of this burden? I would like to see the world with my own eyes again. Before it's too late.

CAL: And as I stared at this woman, I felt this powerful desire to capture her in all her complexity. Somehow, I knew that this would be the last, and only moment, that anyone ever saw Wyatt James alive.

And so, I began to paint.

EPILOGUE

GUANTANAMO BAY NAVAL BASE

Eleven Days After the Competition

CAL: When I pushed stop on the tape recorder, Carrie wiped the tears from her cheeks. I reassured her that I would do my best to tell her truth. The selfie-style confession she posted after leaving the lighthouse was only half the story. It was my job to tell the world everything from beginning to end. She could only nod, the emotions lingering on her face. She was done talking. There was so much I wanted to say. That I was sorry. That I had made so many mistakes. I wanted to tell her that I cared about her, loved her. But I knew it wasn't the right time. Retelling the story drained her. The door buzzed and the two guards walked in to bring her back to her cell. They were about to grab her when I motioned for the guards to stop. There was one more question I needed to ask.

"Was there ever a chance for us?"

Carrie smiled sadly. Then shook her head. "You lost me the moment you abandoned me at that factory," she said. "Just like my brother, you chose what was easy. Your desire for revenge was greater than your love for me. I don't blame you or Tuck. But I deserve better. I deserve more."

I nodded. I understood. She was right.

And then she was escorted out of the room.

AGENT COOPER: The debriefing with Kiana Martin in Havana ended eleven days after the competition. As soon as we finished the interview, she advised us that Wyatt would like to reveal the final piece of his installation. Truthfully, I was a little hesitant. After everything I've heard, who would follow Wyatt's instructions blindly? But we had fifteen agents and a small S.W.A.T. team tagging along. I was in the lead car, Kiana in the backseat. As we drove, Kiana stared eagerly out the window, as if this was all some big game, or a horrific trap we were walking into. Part of me wondered if the SUVs behind us would blow up like you see in the movies. Wyatt James was theatrical after all. But they didn't. We made it to the address.

It was an old church, *Cathedral de Santa Maria*. The building was dilapidated, with crumbling stone and broken stained glass. Kiana led us into the cathedral, flanked by S.W.A.T. The place was being renovated, draped in plastic and scaffolding on all sides. We entered the main chamber. And that's when we saw it…

A recreation of the painting that Bella Allesandra described in her testimony. The one with the women on the beach next to the pirate king. Except instead of paint, it was actual human beings. Ten influencers with shaved heads draped in togas, staring into the abyss like wax figures, yellow blindfolds over their eyes. And in the middle was her, King James, adorned in that signature ski mask. I motioned our team to her side. Guns were drawn. But she didn't move. I asked one of the soldiers to remove her mask.

As soon as we lifted the mask, the guns were withdrawn. The woman known as Wyatt James was dead, with a deep laceration across her neck, her eyes removed from their sockets. We have now determined that Wyatt's real name was Jezebella Torma, a child actress born to Hungarian immigrant parents. They abandoned her in Los Angeles at the age of ten. Many believe Jezabella had many disguises and identities throughout the years, including a personal assistant to the late Kelly Trozzo.

And the influencers?

It took a while to rouse them from their position, and when we did, they almost looked like they were coming out of an extended trance. Most of them came with us quietly.

The report says you found something in that cathedral.

I turned that place upside down looking for clues. Turns out the only clue was on the underside of Wyatt James' mask. Sketched into the cloth was a name of a prominent actor in Hollywood, along with the symbol XIIX.

What was the actor's name?

We are not at liberty to share that information at the moment.

Why would Wyatt James give you a clue?

Perhaps she realized the error in her ways. Perhaps she was trying to help us put an end to this shadowy organization. To find out what they have planned next—this Great Awakening that Kiana spoke of.

Do you have any idea what it all means?

We still don't know how far this conspiracy goes, or what this mysterious entity is, or how many deaths they are responsible for. We know it is a ruthless and powerful organization that has its shadowy hand deep into the heart of Hollywood.

But you believe it's real?

It's very real. And like I said before, I won't stop until I discover the truth.

THREE MONTHS LATER

CARRIE: What do you want to know? I'm Carrie Andrews and I'm the winner of Influencer Island. Recently, I've been cleared by the FBI of all charges against me. My case was simple—self-defense and temporary insanity. That's what it was. I don't want to discuss it any further. Most of the internet agrees with me. My 100 million followers certainly do. It seems that all has been forgiven, even if the occasional meme still floats around the internet. Truthfully, I don't even recognize some of those screenshots taken from the island.

Looking back, are you surprised you chose death when Wyatt presented you with your options?

And what? Become one of Wyatt's cult followers? I don't regret anything. I came to that island broken, and through the process, I rediscovered myself. I am proud to be Carrie Andrews. Looking death straight in the eye is a testament of who my brother made me to be. The difference is, I get a second chance. I'm not going to waste it.

These days, I spend most of my time traveling from one beach to the next, crafting sponsored posts and living out of five-star hotels. My clothing line will be coming out this fall. I'm excited about that. I still don't surf professionally, but I post a few videos here and there to prove that I'm not a complete phony. **[LAUGHS]**

This week, I'm headed out to Bora Bora to surf some waves and meet up with a few influencer friends for a photoshoot promoting this new festival. It'll be fun. The scar on my leg? Everyone wants to talk about the scar. The iron metal of the skull and heart that cauterized my wound. I was going to get a tattoo over it, but I kind of like it. It reminds me of that turning point in my life. That Tuck orchestrated that entire experience. He died so I can live.

Did you ever ask Wyatt where Tuck's body was?

No. It doesn't matter. The painting was enough. I don't need to see him suspended in liquid like Cal's father. Whatever is left of my brother lives on in me.

CAL: My first solo art exhibit will be taking place in three weeks. The main attraction is the Wyatt James piece. I have promised to reveal the face of the most famous artist in the world. Honestly, it's not my favorite. There is so much rage in those brushstrokes. But it's raw and real. My favorite piece is still the one I painted on the island of Carrie. There's something special about that one. I won't sell it. It always makes me smile. Most of my life has been spent living in the past, isolating myself, scared to get close to anyone. That painting reminds me that there is a future. That I want to find somebody and be happy. I don't want to hide like my father or Wyatt James.

I haven't spoken with Carrie. But I invited her to my show. I hope she comes.

CARRIE: I wish I could, but my schedule is booked solid. Am I happy? I don't know. I think so. Late at night, when I scroll through my feed to see all the pictures of myself on faraway beaches, I think, *who wouldn't want this life?* I have fans all over the world. . . Hold on . . . What was the question? Sorry, I've been

DM'ing this actress. Apparently, she wants to play me in a film adaption of my story. It's all so crazy, right?

CAL: As everyone at BlueLA now knows, this will be my last podcast episode. They threw me a great party on my last day. I'm glad my career as a reporter is over. I'm not going to miss it. Working at BlueLA, while fun, was something to distract me from my true calling. I'm thankful for the island. I'm thankful for what it gave me. It reconnected me with what I'm supposed to be doing. I was meant to be an artist.

CARRIE: I think my brother would be proud of me.

CAL: I think my father would have been proud of me.

CARRIE: Yesterday, a photographer took a great photo of me in a swimsuit from my new line to tease the release. Strangely enough, the post only has 68,000 views. I posted a similar one two weeks ago that got 75,000 views, and that was without the teaser announcement. I convinced myself it was the algorithm, always shortening its reach. But there's a tiny seed of doubt in the back of my mind. *What would happen if this all went away?*

[SMILES]

I think I'd be okay.

AGENT COOPER:

Any final takeaways from this investigation?

I learned a lot about human nature during the course of this investigation. It's funny, each and every one of these influencers and contestants knew, to a certain extent, what they were getting into. Regardless, they all stepped onto that plane. They were willing to risk their lives for fame, followers, and influence. They even turned down millions of dollars. So in the end, who was really responsible?

DR KATZ: Was Influencer Island Wyatt James's greatest masterpiece? It's subjective, isn't it? But I believe Wyatt taught us a valuable lesson about the masks we wear. The brands we present to the world. How identities become self-imposed prisons. As human beings, we are not confined to mere products or whatever we place in our digital bios. We are human souls. Complex. Complicated. Most of all, mortal. This future metaverse we speak of; it must account for that.

Now do I believe Wyatt needed to kill innocent kids to prove this point? No. But it's a valid point, nonetheless. As an artist myself, I understand the ambition. In some ways, I applaud the lengths in which she went to make her point. But no. I don't consider it a masterpiece. Who knows what they'll be saying in a decade?

LANE: Was it a masterpiece... Shit, fifty million people tuned in to see the art installation. The Sistine Chapel gets about five million visitors per year. Whatever your opinion is, you can't argue that this was one of the most influential—no pun intended—pieces of artwork ever produced. And it won't hang in a museum. Or be sold at some auction. Influencer Island lives in the cloud. With the digital portraits of the people who died. It lives in everyone that came home from the island. We're still taking about it, aren't we?

JOSS: A final note. Eleven days after the competition aired, every digital portrait by Wyatt James purchased at auction transformed. The images of each model with a gold streak over their eyes glitched, and then became a new portrait altogether. An image of the influencer with a shaved head and a stoic, expressionless face. More notably, the blur was removed, and their eyes were revealed.

Out of all the surviving influencers who were tortured by Wyatt James, all of them have relaunched their Gl!tch accounts. They are also in the process of filming another reality show called *Restore*. In it, the influencers from the island, along with a handful of other male influencers, retreat to a holistic center in Iceland to heal and recover from the experience. The network is spinning it as "Love Island" meets "Goop."

Following the contest and podcast, Bella Allesandra received considerable blowback for her role in what transpired on the island. Bella posted a formal apology on Gl!tch. She also announced that she would be starting a non-profit that promotes body positivity as well as removing the waist-cinching products from her website.

Kiana Martin is currently being held at a correction facility and awaits trial.

Gl!tch CEO Brian Campbell was forced to testify in front of Congress to answer for his platform's role in the contest. In his testimony, Campbell stated that Gl!tch wasn't necessarily good or bad, but a neutral application that promotes freedom of speech. To temper public outrage, Campbell promised to add a feature that removed likes and follower count from individual profiles. Ninety-nine percent of users ignore this feature.

Sidenote: Two months after we got a final statement from Carrie, she made a post saying that she is on a "digital detox" and has not made a single post in over a month. In a recent paparazzi photo, Cal and Carrie were spotted at a café in Los Angeles. Neither of them has commented on their relationship.

As for me, I have been promoted to executive producer at BlueLA studios. My team and I can't wait to share what we have planned next. Thank you for listening. We hope that you enjoyed this podcast. Stay tuned for more!

ALSO BY KYLE RUTKIN

For a preview of the next book

Go to diedfamousbooks.com/eleven

Other novels in the Died Famous Universe

She Died Famous

Tik Tik Gone - Prequel to Influencer Island

Sign up for the email list diedfamous.substack.com

ACKNOWLEDGMENTS

The inspiration behind this book was—You guessed it—Fyre Festival. I started and stopped this book idea about a dozen times. But no matter how much I worked on it, the voice never felt right. It was only when I started listening to true crime podcasts (along with reading World War Z) did the voice finally come to me.

Thank you to my family, especially my wife and two daughters for being my continual source of inspiration.

Thank you to everyone who looked at a first edition, including all my ARC readers.

Thank you to my editor, Julie Tibbott.

Thank you to my wonderful designer, Anamaria Stefan for bringing the Died Famous universe to life. Your design work on *She Died Famous* was part of the inspiration behind this book. That wonderful yellow blur needed a true origin story.

Thank you to my family for supporting and buying my books even when they are not your cup of tea. Sorry they keep coming out dark! ;)

Thank you to Bookstagram and BookTok for all that you do for new authors, especially indie authors. I truly believe we are living in the greatest era of publishing. Platforms like TikTok allow readers to decide what will be the next bestseller. So, share your story. Write the story on your heart. You never know who's going to pick it up.

Someone out there needs your story!

Made in the USA
Monee, IL
01 January 2023

24109356R00111